SHADOW MAN

VB/CGL

SHADOW MAN

His name was Calvin Taylor but the Apaches called him Shadow Man. Now he was the guide for a wagon train of down-on-their-luck farmers following the Trail of Lost Souls, but the trail became a journey of death and Taylor found himself branded a renegade. Only a man with his peculiar talent for making enemies could find himself in the saddle of the bitter war between white man and Apache, being hunted by both sides. He was pursued across a strange land by Loco's Mescaleros and by the real renegade whose deadly secret Taylor might reveal.

SHADOW MAN

by

Andrew McBride

Dales Large Print Books
Long Preston, North Yorkshire,
BD23 4ND, England.

British Library Cataloguing in Publication Data.

McBride, Andrew
    Shadow man.

    A catalogue record of this book is
    available from the British Library

    ISBN   978-1-84262-715-0 pbk

First published in Great Britain in 2008 by Robert Hale Limited

Copyright © Andrew McBride 2008

Cover illustration © Gordon Crabb by arrangement with
Alison Eldred

The right of Andrew McBride to be identified as the author of
this work has been asserted by him in accordance with the
Copyright, Designs and Patents Act, 1988

Published in Large Print 2009 by arrangement with
Robert Hale Ltd.

Dales Large Print is an imprint of Library Magna Books Ltd.

Printed and bound in Great Britain by
T.J. (International) Ltd., Cornwall, PL28 8RW

Thanks to K P., A.M., and (especially) Philip Davenport; in tribute to the man who made *Wagon Master*.

CHAPTER ONE

Buzzards turned in the sky.

They planed on brown-grey wings, cutting slow, tightening circles. They might have been tethered by an invisible leash to a spot on the desert floor far below.

That told Calvin Taylor a little. Something down there was hurt but it was still alive, otherwise the buzzards would be spiralling down to feed.

Taylor sat his grey horse in the only cover hereabouts: the shade between two large boulders. He lifted field glasses to his eyes and studied the land to the east.

The green country, the valley of the Rio Grande, was behind him. Ahead was only a seared and waterless landscape, all the way to the Pecos River: Southern New Mexico Territory. Mountain ranges that paralleled each other, trending north to south. Between these ranges were desert basins. The nearest range, the Lagarto Mountains, lay before him. The Lagartos were well-named, dim, lizard-like shapes with a spine like the edge of a saw running against the sky. Beyond them lay his destination: the new mining camp of Ore City.

Through his field glasses Taylor studied the carrion birds overhead and then the ground they staked out. He frowned. The buzzards hovered over the first foothills of the Lagartos, where there was a sight too much cover for his liking. It would be safer and wiser to keep to open country. Nonetheless Taylor kneed his horse in the ribs and rode towards the place the buzzards marked.

The wind brought suffocating waves of heat, and fine, warm dust that scratched his skin. It was only early June and already as hot as hell's griddle.

Calvin Taylor was twenty-five years old. He was six feet tall, and of medium build; a good-looking young man with dark hair and, in contrast, very blue eyes. He had grown a moustache to put some age in his face and wore two days of patchy trail beard. His clothing was functional, not stylish. The colour had long faded from his Levis and flannel shield-front shirt. He wore an equally faded poncho he'd bought in the last town along the way – Paso Del Norte – and a battered plainsman's hat. He carried a long-barrelled Colt .44 pistol in a cross-draw holster on his left hip and a fifteen-shot Winchester, model of 1873, in the saddle boot on his horse. A knife was sheathed on his right hip. All this weaponry was a considerable burden on man and horse but they were necessary. Even now, in 1879, this was still dangerous country.

Taylor rode slowly across a plain of low brush – saltbrush, creosote, clumps of yucca – under the eye of the sun and in the teeth of the hot wind. Haze blurred the horizons and turned the lizard spine of the mountains to wave crests, rippling towards some far shore. This was high desert and altitude made the air burn his lungs. It was very silent. It was still, too; then a white dust showed, streaking across the desert face, pelting away from him.

Taylor had his hand to his rifle and the Winchester halfway out of its boot before he realized this was only the strange ground-running bird called the chaparral cock fleeing before him. He told himself, 'You're getting jumpy, Taylor.'

He could see a cleft in the wall of foothills before him, a little narrow canyon angling in there, towards the place the buzzards marked. He decided only a damn fool would leave open ground and enter those hills, where he could be trapped and ambushed easy as you please. But curiosity was pulling on him and he rode into the canyon. It was his day to be a damn fool.

He made one concession to common sense: he drew his Winchester from its boot, cocked it, and laid it across the saddle before him.

Rock walls rose on either side, bare and sheer. The heat trapped between had no air to stir it, was solid, dizzying. The canyon crooked ahead, angling out of sight. Brush and haze provided a myriad hiding-places all around him. Taylor decided he'd been fool enough for one day. He'd turn his horse about, quit this canyon and leave the buzzards to their work.

Taylor was conscious of a ledge, shouldering out of the rock wall behind and above him and how close he'd let himself get to it. He began to knee his horse forward. Then something clattered on the trail before him. Taylor looked that way. In the same instant he caught movement in the corner of his eye. A man was suddenly standing on the ledge!

This man ran forward, yelling.

And sprang.

As the man leaped towards him, Taylor swung his horse about. He lashed out with the rifle in his hand.

The barrel struck home; the plunging figure grunted and was flung aside. The blow pulled Taylor to the left, half out of the saddle. At the same time his horse jumped to the right. Suddenly Taylor had no horse under him. He seemed to hang in the air an instant; then he struck the ground very hard, on his front.

By good luck he came down on a slope of white sand, but the fall still knocked most of the air out of his lungs. He lay prone for a time, trying to find breath. He tasted the harshness of gypsum in his mouth. The glare of salt-white earth hurt his eyes.

Slowly he sat up.

His attacker lay on the slope above. He moved slowly too, coming to all fours, then kneeling up.

Taylor saw a man in a faded red polka-dot shirt and muslin loin-cloth, now fouled with white dust. His very black, chest length hair was tied across the temples with a thick band of red calico. A chevron of white bottomclay banded his face from ear to ear, running across the bridge of the nose, startling against his dark-copper skin. He got to his feet and showed he was bare-legged behind the breech-clout, wearing crumpled knee-

13

high moccasins. He had a knife in his hand.

An Apache.

Dazedly, Taylor became aware of the Winchester lying on the earth before him. He got his hands to it.

The Apache charged.

As he ran he put the knife between his teeth. Taylor scrambled upright, lifting the rifle and the Indian seized it with both hands, cannoning into Taylor and driving him backwards. Taylor fell and rolled down the slope; the Apache spilled over him and rolled too. They tumbled down-slope in dust.

Where the slope levelled, they floundered in this choking stuff. Taylor got to a crouch, looking around for his rifle and a dim shape loomed over him. A man with a knife in his hand, striking down.

Taylor dodged and grabbed the man's arm. He yanked, turning as he did so, pitching the Indian headlong over his right shoulder. The Apache somersaulted forward, striking on his back. Taylor sprang in on him. The Apache kicked up from the ground. His foot went into Taylor's belly, hooking Taylor into the air. Taylor performed his own neat somersault and crashed down on loose sand.

The Indian lunged at him again but he

was slower. Taylor had time to get to his knees. As the Apache stabbed down, Taylor grabbed his arm. The white man squirmed to his feet. He was six inches taller than the Indian, but they seemed matched for strength. The knife point was only a few inches from Taylor's throat; he strained to hold it there. They swayed, locked together, each one's hands to the other's wrists, almost face to face. The Apache's teeth were bared in a snarl, very white against his dark skin.

Suddenly the expression of ferocity on the Indian's face changed. It became pain. A sigh came out of him. All the strength seemed to leach out of him at once; he sank down. Taylor lifted his foot, placing it against the Indian's chest, and kicked out. The man was driven backwards, sprawling on the slope.

Taylor reached down and lifted the Winchester. The Apache had dropped his knife. Taylor snatched that up too. He found he was dizzy with weariness after only a few minutes' physical exertion in this heat. Breath panted out of him. His arms trembled as they always did after violent action. Sweat was running into his eyes. He wiped it away and took aim on the man lying before him.

The Apache sat up, making small sounds

of pain. That was explained when he reached behind him, putting his hand to his back. His fingers came away bloody. There were blood patches on the white sand around him. He looked up at Taylor calmly, in his face a sullen acceptance of his death.

This was a young man, younger than his white enemy. After a moment Taylor recognized him. In Apache (which he spoke well) Taylor said, 'Hello Nachay. You got a bullet in you?'

The wounded man was trying to keep his face a mask, Taylor could see that; it was something an Indian could do easily, but for an instant the mask slipped and he looked puzzled. Nachay said, 'I remember you from the agency. You're the one they call Shadow Man.'

Nachay meant Rat, but that wasn't an insult in Nachay's world. Apaches honoured the rat as a clever animal. Taylor told him: 'I always figured your daddy, Loco, was a pretty smart Indian. So why'd he leave the reservation?'

'The white eyes promised to feed us on the reservation. But you can't eat promises. They wanted to starve us like they did the Navajos.' About ten years back, Taylor knew, the white man had penned up the Navajos on the Bosque Redondo, where thousands of them had died of starvation, hunger and disease. Nachay's eyes moved to the rifle in Taylor's hand. 'Better to die like an Apache.'

'I'm not going to kill you, Nachay.'

'Why not? I'd kill you.'

'There's been enough killing. Tell your daddy to come in and talk peace.'

Nachay was struggling to keep the shield over his face and not let his further puzzlement show. Taylor turned away from him and began to climb the slope towards his horse. He'd taken half a dozen paces when Nachay said, 'Shadow Man!'

Taylor turned back. Nachay was on his feet. He held out something, a strip of some material. Nachay said, 'If you come across any of my people, show them this. It might keep you alive.'

Taylor took this object. It was a belt of maybe dried pony skin, daubed with crude paintings of horses, deer, the moon and stars and symbols he didn't recognize.

He said, '*Adios*, Nachay.'

Taylor tied the Apache belt to his horse's bridle and swung into the saddle. Nachay stood watching him. The Indian's eyes burned holes in Taylor's back as he rode out of the canyon.

CHAPTER TWO

Ore City was as ugly as its name. Once it had been a tiny Mexican hamlet of fifteen or so adobes grouped around just enough space to stage a cockfight. But the mines had come, and the Anglos determined to tear their fortune from the earth. After that, Ore City had grown too quickly to be pretty. Now it was a raw settlement climbing hills on both sides of an almost dry creek. A haphazard scatter of dwellings of all kinds: brush huts, adobes, frame structures, false-fronted buildings, tents, together with bizarre hybrids of adobe, wood and canvas. Despite its grand title it wasn't quite city size yet. Perhaps a thousand people might live in this neighbourhood, though many were invisible most of the time. They burrowed away in the mines that gave this place its name and its reason to exist.

Calvin Taylor came into Ore City from the west, along the Paso Del Norte trail. It was only about 11 a.m. but stamp mills thumped away in the hills. Doubtless they worked round the clock. He noted that there only seemed to be two buildings above one-storey size in view. One was a hotel. The other, a vast barnlike structure had a sign over one doorway bearing the legend: GENERAL MERCHANDISE. J. GARTH PROPRIETOR.

Taylor reined in at a horse trough in front of this building and dismounted. He tied his horse at a hitching rail away from the water. Then he moved to the trough and proceeded to wash his face. The water was warm and not too clean but he didn't care. He unknotted his bandanna and used it to towel his face dry. As he did so a man came out of the store carrying two sacks of flour, which he placed in the back of a buckboard.

Taylor said, 'Morning.'

The other man smiled. It was the ready smile of a businessman to whom any stranger was a potential customer. 'Morning. Hot one, ain't it?' He wore an apron that was bleached with flour dust. There was dust on his hands too. He wiped some of that away, then extended one hand. 'Garth is the name.'

Taylor heard the Southern hill country – Tennessee, Arkansas – in Garth's soft accent, which meant he came from the same part of

19

the world as Taylor himself. Taylor intro-
duced himself, they shook. Taylor was
surprised at the power in Garth's grip, his
fingers like iron. Garth was about Taylor's
height, and of slim build. He was in his
forties, a handsome man with a long, narrow
face, fashionable handlebar moustache and a
little grey at the temples of his dark hair. His
was a humorous, good-living face, and
deeply tanned for a storekeeper who presumably spent most of his time indoors.

Now that his horse had cooled down
Taylor let the animal drink from the trough.
He said, 'Supposed to be a wagon train in
this neighbourhood.'

A little surprise showed in Garth's eyes.
'You mean those crazy fools fixing to go
down to the Rio Azul?' When Taylor nodded
slightly, Garth said, 'They're camped on the
other side of town, along the creek there.'

Taylor swung up into the saddle. 'Much
obliged.'

Garth dampened his hands in the trough
and started to wipe more flour dust from
him, smiling again; then his gaze sharpened
on something. The smile slipped from his
lips.

Taylor realized he'd left Nachay's gift, the
strip of pony hide, hanging from his bridle.

Garth reached forward and touched it. 'Where'd you get this Apache gewgaw?'

'Traded it from a friendly Indian.' Which was an approximation to the truth, Taylor decided.

Garth glared at the horseman. All the humour and friendliness were gone from his face. His eyes, which ought to have been dark but were grey, had anger in them. His mouth twisted with contempt. 'Friendly Indian.'

Garth spat. Maybe he spat at Taylor's boot. If so he only missed by inches, the spittle coiling on the earth by the horse's front hoofs.

Taylor found himself in a staring contest with the older man. After a little of that, Taylor glanced up at the sign over the door, wondering how he'd been so slow as not to register the name. 'You Jedediah Garth, by any chance?'

'You heard of me?'

Taylor didn't answer. He turned his horse and rode down the street.

He'd heard of Garth all right. If Garth had known that Taylor had let the son of Loco live, when he could have killed him, he'd probably have gone to his gun then and there. In a territory of Indian-haters, Jed Garth had a reputation all of his own.

Thinking of that, Taylor reached down and untied the Apache belt from around his horse's bridle and stuffed it into a saddle-bag.

He rode by saloons that were clearly doing fair business even at this early hour. He was tempted to cut the dust but resisted. He was about to meet his new employers and didn't want to do so with whiskey on his breath.

Buildings thinned around him and he came to the edge of the desert and to a creek, a riffle of brown water maybe two feet deep and twenty paces across. It looped about, its banks lined in places with stunted trees, cottonwoods and such, a belt of green on land that had most of the colour burned out of it. Covered wagons were drawn up in a loose circle on the far side. Taylor could see mules and oxen grazing further down the creek. People were about, men, women and children.

Taylor rode across the creek. Ahead of him a small mesquite fire burned, a spider over it and a coffee pot on that. A woman in an apron and white dress with some kind of brown pattern on it stood by the fire.

She looked up as Taylor approached, shading her eyes with her hand so that he couldn't see her face.

Taylor touched the brim of his hat. He said, 'Morning, ma'am. I'm looking for Major Cameron.'

A voice behind him asked: 'Who wants me?'

Taylor turned to see a man striding towards him.

Alexander Cameron was in his mid-fifties, Taylor judged. He was large and barrel-chested, standing a few inches over six feet. He was hatless, his florid, slablike face topped with a thatch of iron-grey hair. Cameron went in for burnsides and a heavy walrus moustache which was whiter than his hair. He walked with his lower lip and his chin jutting forward. It was a pugnacious face, but not without humour.

Taylor told him: 'Seems like I'm your guide, Major.'

Cameron blinked. 'You're Calvin Taylor?' He frowned. 'I was expecting an older man.'

'I'm older than I look.'

Cameron fingered one of his burnsides. 'Just how old are you, exactly?' Taylor heard a faint Scots burr, far back in his voice.

'Twenty-six.' Which was almost the truth; Taylor would be in a matter of weeks.

The Scotsman's gaze remained sceptical. Taylor became aware that others around the wagons were staring at him too. Faces were doubtful. It seemed that everyone was glaring and frowning at him today.

One man stepped forward. He asked Taylor, 'You're going to be our guide into bad country?'

'That's right.'

The man smiled very slightly. A little contempt came into his voice. 'You sure don't look old enough to me.'

This was a man of about thirty. He stood a little above middle height but his broad chest and bull shoulders made him seem taller. His hair was dark and his moustache luxuriant, a vanity. A very handsome man, with a hint of arrogance in his face that suggested he knew it. He wore drab work clothes that had a lot of dust on them. His only affectation was the gloves he wore, thick gauntlets with long fringes at the sides.

Cameron's voice came. 'Now, Evans...'

Evans glanced over at the major. 'Yes sir?'

'My cousin up at Val Verde recommended Taylor here. That's good enough for me.'

Evans began to speak, maybe to argue, but then he held his tongue. After a moment he walked away.

Cameron told Taylor, 'Don't mind Buck Evans. He's kind of prickly, sometimes. Will you join us in a cup of coffee, sir?'

Taylor swung down from the saddle. He and Cameron shook hands. Whilst the Scot had larger hands than Garth, his grip was easier. Cameron indicated the woman in the white dress. 'This is my daughter, Fiona.'

She stood against the sun; he couldn't make her out clearly, save that she was fair-haired. 'Ma'am.'

She held out a cup of coffee to him, which he took. 'Thank you.'

The woman moved away. Taylor squatted down, getting comfortable on his hunkers. He drank the hot, unsugared coffee grate-fully. 'When you fixing to pull out, Major?'

'You come straight to the point,' Cameron observed. 'Good. Now you're here, we can pull out tomorrow morning.'

'All right. After this–' Taylor raised his coffee cup, '–I'm going over to the hotel to book a room for tonight and bathe some of this desert off me. Around three, four, I'll mosey back over here and give your wagons a look over. Gives you time to change your mind about this trip.'

Cameron gave him a sharp look. 'Why should we change our minds?'

'Because Loco has jumped the reserv-ation.'

The Scot poured himself some coffee. 'I've heard all about these Apache renegades.'

'The Mescaleros used to hide out in the Superstition Mountains. That's close by where you're fixing to go.'

'Talk is they've run off to Mexico.'

Remembering Nachay, Taylor felt unease. He frowned. 'Maybe. Maybe not. Might be wiser to wait and see.'

It was Cameron's turn to frown. He fingered one burnside. This was clearly a habit with him, an aid to thinking. 'Quite frankly, Mr Taylor, we can't afford to wait. Most of us have put everything we have into outfitting for this trip. We're eating into what's left of our money and supplies as it is. We need to get down to the Rio Azul while there's still time to put crops in. So I don't intend to linger here just because Loco *might* be in that country.'

'As long as you know what you might be getting into. Even without hostiles, it's pretty mean country all the way to Rio Azul.'

'But once we get there, it's paradise.'

Taylor glanced up at Cameron in surprise. Nobody who had been along the Rio Azul would ever describe it as paradise. Taylor wondered if he should tell Cameron that brutal truth now. But he was hired as a scout, nothing else. It wasn't his place to stamp on this man's hopes and illusions. 'Well, at least it'll grow something, unlike the rest of this country.'

'You changing *your* mind?'

Taylor finished his coffee, threw the grounds to the earth. 'You're paying me, Major.'

He stood and moved to his horse.

As he climbed into the saddle he saw Fiona Cameron standing nearby, watching him. Now he could see her clearly, Taylor decided she was strikingly attractive, maybe even beautiful. Perhaps twenty-three. She was tall with a lot of golden hair – some might consider it a sinful amount – piled up on her head. Her cotton dress was long enough to allow no glimpse of ankle, but it couldn't hide her shapely figure and full breasts. Some might think her eyes – which were of a colour he couldn't quite identify – and mouth were sinful too.

He said, 'Thanks for the coffee, ma'am.'

He rode towards town.

Buck Evans was suddenly in his path. Taylor reined in.

Evans stared up at the horseman whilst fondling the fringes at the side of his gloves.

His eyes were disdainful. He dawdled a minute or so, in no hurry to give the other man the road. Then he stepped aside and Taylor rode by.

Taylor decided he hadn't lost his knack of making enemies at the drop of a hat. First Garth and now Evans. Maybe taking on this job was a mistake, and he should let Cameron find himself another trailblazer. Almost certainly he'd have to whip Evans to get these movers to accept him as a scout. He thought about the strength in the man's arms and shoulders. He thought about the killing look in Jed Garth's eyes. And then he thought about Fiona Cameron's eyes, which might be green...

CHAPTER THREE

Next morning, an hour after daybreak, the wagons were lined one after another along the creek, pointing east.

Taylor had carried out his inspection the previous afternoon ('Ma'am, you won't get a stove that heavy ten miles down the trail we're following.') and had given the wagons a further looking over just now. He squatted by a mesquite fire, finishing up a breakfast of bacon and beans on the tin plate on his lap. Breakfast courtesy of Fiona Cameron.

He felt depressed.

The train consisted of ten wagons. The four Williams brothers owned a Conestoga, which looked too big and unwieldy for the country they proposed to travel. The others were the lighter, smaller 'prairie schooners'. Most of the wagons were in fair condition, although the mixture of oxen and mules pulling them were gaunt and ribshot. The outfit was low on saddle horses and most of them were fairly worn down.

There were thirty-six people, eighteen of

them men or boys old enough to use a gun. All of them were farmers who'd come down from Kansas, except a Mexican woman – Señora Sanchez and her fifteen-year-old half-Zuni son who had joined the train in the last few weeks. Mercifully there were only two families with children – an Irishman called McShane had a small tribe of kids underfoot – and the Veidts, a Dutch or German family, who had three young ones, and who knew scarcely one word of English.

Some of the older men had served in the War but none of them had fought Indians, except for Buck Evans and his younger brother Ethan. The Evans brothers had tried their hand at buffalo hunting and had fought Comanches on the High Plains. Or so they claimed. They were armed with Winchesters, as was Major Cameron. The others were armed with a ragbag of weapons, down to the Dutchers who had only one Colt pistol between them. (Taylor had insisted they get themselves a rifle.)

The size of the outfit, as well as their lack of experience in Indian fighting, added to Taylor's gloom. They were too big to escape notice, yet not big enough to withstand a large war party, especially if the Apaches spotted how poorly armed they were. Any bronco Apache's mouth would water at the prospect of the booty on this train – guns, ammunition, supplies, oxen and mules, not to mention women and children to be carried off as slaves. And there weren't just Apaches to consider. There were bandits in this country – and across the line in Mexico, who could plunder as ruthlessly as any Apache. In the past bands of them had wiped out wagon trains and made it look as though Indians had done it.

Of course, if there were no human enemies to threaten them, then all the travellers might have to endure was heat, thirst and dust. But you couldn't bank on that. Taylor finished his breakfast, mopping up bacon grease with a sourdough biscuit. He remembered the faces of the wagon party as he'd moved amongst them. Faces marked with weariness, disappointment and defeat, faces without hope. Worn-down people in worn-down clothes. That depressed him too. He wondered again about taking on this job. Maybe he ought to spell out to Cameron the realities of what he'd find on the Rio Azul, then quit and let the major get himself another scout.

He finished breakfast, ate dessert – an apple – and rolled a cornshuck cigarette.

Major Cameron approached, smiling.

'Well,' he asked, 'Are we ready to roll?'

Taylor lit his cigarette. 'Just about. Thank your daughter for a fine breakfast.'

Cameron poured himself coffee.

Taylor said, 'You're still set on this trip? I think you're crazy.'

His bluntness drew an angry glare from Cameron, who held that look for a minute. Then his face became weary. He said, 'I don't mean to sound patronizing but as a young man you perhaps can't appreciate what it means to be busted down to nothing. To work hard all your life and then have it snatched away from you. You grind away for years and years and then lose it all in ... days.' Cameron paused, presumably remembering hard times. He looked bleak, his face suddenly that of an old man. 'We farmed in Kansas and grasshoppers did for us. Ate all our crops two years running. In Nebraska it was drought. So we set out for California but the money ran out. Left us stranded here. Then we heard about the new settlements at Rio Azul. So you see, Mr Taylor, we're at the end of the trail. Literally. Rio Azul is the last throw of the dice – for all of us.'

Taylor heard the despair in the man's

voice. Despite himself he felt oddly moved.

He threw the remnants of his cigarette to the earth and stood. 'I'll get 'em going.'

Within half an hour the wagons were manned and drivers poised to crack their whips and get the stock rolling. A hot east wind lifted, sifting dust across, so they'd move with dust blowing into their faces. The wind flapped canvas and pulled at the men's hats and the women's sunbonnets.

Taylor and Cameron sat their horses at the front of the train. They gazed into the glare of the desert beyond.

Cameron lifted his battered slouch hat from his head and used it to shade his eyes. 'If there's a trail out there, I can't see it.'

Taylor narrowed his eyes against the wind. 'It ain't much. They say the Spaniards first used it a couple hundred years back. A big expedition, soldiers and priests and such. They called it the Trail of Hope cus it was supposed to lead to a city of gold. When they found out it didn't lead anywhere, they renamed it the Trail of Lost Souls.'

Cameron smiled a very little. 'Still trying to get me to change my mind? Maybe it'll turn into our Trail of Hope.'

'Maybe.'

Cameron slewed around in the saddle and faced the wagons behind him. He lifted his arm. In his strong voice he bellowed: 'Let's go!' With his arm he gestured forward and the lead wagon began to move, the others following. Fiona drove the Cameron wagon. The prairie schooners – and the Williams's Conestoga – wobbled and crawled out of Ore City, on to the Trail of Lost Souls.

A small crowd had gathered at the edge of town and watched the wagons leave. Amongst them was a tall man in a black shirt, who seemed to have his eyes fixed on Taylor. As he rode by Taylor saw that this man was Jedediah Garth.

CHAPTER FOUR

When the wagons reached their first nooning place, and the travellers were taking their meal, Calvin Taylor gathered the handful of men with saddle horses before him. That included the two Evans brothers and the four Williams siblings. It also included the half-Zuni boy, Ramon Sanchez.

Taylor told the men standing before him: 'From now on, four outriders out at all times. Point, rear and flanks.' Buck was staring off at the wagons. Taylor asked, 'You listening, Evans?' Evans started as if Taylor had flicked him with a quirt. He glared. Taylor ignored that and went on: 'The most dangerous is rear.'

After a little discussion they picked the first four outriders and worked out a rota for who followed them. Then Taylor broke up the meeting. He hunkered down and started to roll a cigarette. As he might have predicted, Buck Evans was the one to linger behind when the others walked away.

Evans told Taylor, 'I don't like the idea of

having that Sanchez kid as an outrider.'

'Why not?'

'He's an Indian. Apaches around, more likely he'll join them than warn us.'

'He's part Zuni, not Apache.'

'Same breed of cats.'

Taylor felt a flicker of temper. He made his voice rougher than it needed to be. 'Shows you don't know anything about Indians. Apaches and Zunis was enemies before white men even got out here.'

A little anger showed in Evans's face. 'I know about Indians. When we was buffalo hunting, Ethan and me, we had us a partner. One morning we found him, come on him sudden. Comanches had ... scalped him, cut him up. Cut off his...' Evans voice trailed away, and his lips tightened. He bunched his fists and then slowly flexed his fingers. 'Cut him up something awful. And that was a good man. Five years and I still can't get what I saw out of my head.'

Taylor waited a moment before speaking. 'I'm sorry about that, Evans, but—'

'So don't tell me I don't know about Indians. I seen plenty. They're all the same to me. The only good ones ... well, you know.' He sneered. 'And don't be talking to me like I'm some sort of a kid. I don't have

36

to take your orders.'

Taylor had been moved by Evans' words a moment before, but now temper worked in him again. 'Yes you do. Long as Major Cameron wants me as scout, you'll take my orders and like it!'

Evans blinked. 'Will I now?'

He began to pull off his fringed gloves.

Taylor heard himself sigh. He thought: It might as well be now as later. He stood.

For the first time Evans smiled slightly, a pleasant prospect in front of him.

Then his expression changed, his gaze moving past Taylor, fixing on something.

Fiona Cameron approached. She said, 'Gentlemen.'

Evans touched the brim of his hat. 'Miss Cameron.'

She gave him a brilliant smile. 'You'll come to supper, Buck?'

Evans was suddenly a gentleman mindful of his manners. He pulled his hat off and turned it in his hands. 'I'd be proud to, ma'am.'

Fiona then gave Taylor the same smile. He waited for her invitation to supper too; but it didn't come. She walked away.

Evans gazed after the woman, smiling. Then his eyes moved to Taylor and the smile faded. A vaguely triumphant look replaced it. He strode off.

Taylor was, not for the first time, mystified by a woman's doings. What was all that about? Was Fiona trying to make him jealous? Had she succeeded? Or was she about some strange coquettish game? She needed to be careful, he thought, playing him against Evans when there was already bad feeling between them. A game like that could turn deadly fairly quickly.

The wagons made twenty miles that day. They saw no Indians, few travellers of any kind. The main enemy the travellers faced was the hot wind that blew all day and the alkali dust it raised, rasping skin, bleaching clothes and flesh, greying hair and tasting harshly in the food they ate and the coffee they drank.

At sundown Taylor rode in from his final scout, checked on the night guards, then rode to the circled wagons. As he dismounted there, a figure shaped out of the gathering darkness and came towards him: Ramon Sanchez. Taylor asked him: *'Qué tal, hombre?'*

Ramon shrugged. Most of the time he was too shy to speak or even look you in the eye. Taylor said, 'Your turn on night guard, *amigo*.'

Taylor watched him walk away. Ramon's dark skin, very black hair and high cheekbones showed his Indian blood but at least his hair was cut short and he dressed in the serape and white cotton pants of a Mexican peasant. Otherwise someone might mistake him for an Apache in this darkness and take a shot at him.

The travellers sat around campfires, finishing supper. Taylor found a fire to sit by and ate a tortilla with a beef jerky filling he didn't taste. He was conscious of his own weariness; he'd been how many hours in the saddle today?

It seemed very quiet. Taylor had expected some display of optimism and eagerness from these pilgrims after successfully completing the first day of their journey to the promised land. But there was little activity around the campfires. No Bible meeting or debating, no fiddle or squeezebox music or dancing. Voices were low. Even the children were listless and silent. Maybe heat and dust and the trail had beaten them down. Perhaps this desert and the dangers it might contain had cowed them. With full darkness and the first chill of the desert night, most of them stole away to their beds.

A few campfires remained, burning low.

By one Joshua Williams teased a mournful tune out of a mouth organ.

Someone approached; Taylor looked up and saw Fiona Cameron. She held out a tin cup.

'You seem to like my coffee.'

'Thanks.'

Taylor drank gratefully. 'You sure make good coffee, ma'am.'

He was pleased to see her smile slightly at the compliment. Then he remembered she was just about to eat supper with Buck Evans. Maybe that was a pang of jealousy he felt, after all...

Taylor listened to night noises: Josh Williams's plaintive mouth organ and the lowing of oxen. Far off he could hear coyotes and owls and once the flesh-crawling yowl of a wolf. Real critters, or Apaches impersonating them? He noticed the woman watching him.

She said, 'I was wondering...'

'Yes?'

Fiona gave a small, embarrassed smile. 'I'm forgetting my manners. You don't ask people about their past out here.'

'What were you wondering?'

'Desperation's driven us into this wilderness. But you...'

'Why am I here?' Taylor sipped coffee.

'Maybe I'm a real bad man running from the law.'

She raised an eyebrow. 'Are you?'

Taylor smiled ruefully. 'My story's common enough. I wanted to dig my fortune out of the ground.'

'You were a miner?'

'A prospector. I went looking for gold and silver on my own.'

'Did you find any?'

'No. But I'm still looking.'

Fiona smiled guardedly.

Taylor hadn't told her the whole of his story, but maybe that was enough for now. He said, 'An Apache once asked me: "Why do you come into our country to scratch our rocks? Is it because they itch?"'

She smiled again, more easily this time. 'I didn't know Apaches had a sense of humour.'

'Indians are human beings. Even Apaches.'

'Even this savage, Loco? That means crazy, doesn't it?'

'Other Apaches called him that. They thought he was crazy because he believed you could trust the white man.'

Another smile worked at her lips. 'The Apache sense of humour again?'

'It was Loco who persuaded his band to

41

quit fighting and go on the reservation. Only the whites forgot the promises they'd made to them to get 'em to surrender. They let 'em starve. So Loco broke out, with what was left of his people, rather than see 'em turn into a pack of beggars and drunks. No wonder he's plenty mad right now. He's been played for a sucker. He thinks he's betrayed his people.'

Taylor was a little surprised at the length of the spiel he'd launched, and the vehemence of his tone. Fiona looked surprised by it too.

Taylor said, 'I better watch out. Anyone catches me making speeches like that, they'll call me an Indian lover.' Which he was, literally. A few years back, in Arizona, he'd lived with an Aravaipa Apache girl. But that was another aspect of his story he didn't need to share with Fiona Cameron just yet...

She said, 'But they're cruel aren't they, in war? And treacherous.'

'Sometimes. But so are white men.'

A slight awkwardness came between them. Eventually she said, 'Well, my father's waiting for his supper...'

He watched her walk off towards her wagon. She'd reminded him Buck Evans was waiting for his supper too...

Buck Evans stood in the shadows, listening.

He was dressed in his finest for supper. He wore his best suit of go-to-meeting clothes (his *only* suit of go-to-meeting clothes), had slicked down his hair with the last of his bay rum, shaved as fine as he could manage with his dulled cut-throat razor and polished his boots. He even contemplated presenting Fiona with a bouquet of flowers but decided that was too forward. Besides the only flowers round here were tough desert shrubs, decked with thorns.

He walked towards the Cameron wagon, whistling a tune he'd picked up on the buffalo range. He felt good. Then he saw dim figures standing by a small fire, and heard Fiona's voice, and Calvin Taylor's.

He halted in shadows where he knew he couldn't be seen.

He heard Fiona say, 'I didn't know Apaches had a sense of humour,' and Taylor reply, 'Indians are human beings.' Taylor went on, more Indian-loving nonsense in the same vein.

An image suddenly flashed into Evans's mind. He was labouring up a rise, in his face the ceaseless wind of the Staked Plains. He topped the rise and before him was a little gully, and in that gully lay his partner, Billy Russell. Russell had been stripped naked, his flesh as white as a fish's belly. Evans had squinted against the harsh sunlight of these high, treeless plains and then had come the shock of seeing Russell clearly, seeing what the Comanches had done to him.

Evans came out of his memories, back to the here and now. Taylor and Fiona talked some more, then she walked away from Taylor's fire. She came towards Evans who stepped out of shadows so she could see him.

'Can I walk you to your wagon, Miss Fiona?'

'Surely.'

As they walked along, he said, 'That Taylor...You ever wonder why he knows so much about Indians?' When she didn't reply he asked, 'Do you know what a squaw man is?'

'Is that what he is?'

'More than likely.' That brought no response either and Evans felt a flicker of irritation. He said, 'Just something to keep in mind.'

'My business is my business, Buck.'

'I'm getting a little confused,' he said, 'about what's your business and what's my business.'

She gave him a cool look. 'There's no need to be.'

'You did invite me to supper.'

'That's right. And you're late.'

He felt his temper start to fray. He opened his mouth to give an angry response; then they were at the Cameron wagon.

Fiona had cooked a fine supper but the occasion wasn't a success. Although everyone was scrupulously polite and pleasant there was a frostiness between him and Fiona that never thawed. He walked back to his wagon feeling thwarted and angry. He decided Fiona was toying with him, maybe playing him against Taylor, and he was annoyed at himself for letting that get to him.

Temper had always been Evans's weakness. It had led him to the one thing he'd done of which he was … ashamed might not be the right word. Maybe haunted by.

Out on the buffalo range one night, when everyone was tired and dirty and sick of the stink of a buffalo camp, worn down to their nerve-ends by the constant threat of lurking Comanches, tempers had flared. His *temper* had flared. He'd got into a fight with a fellow named Kolvig, he couldn't remember what about. Kolvig was a weaselly character

with shifty eyes, not clean even by the stan-
dards of buffalo hunters, someone nobody
liked. He was a Polack or Russian with
barely any English so it was hard to imagine
what could have been said that started
things. But start they did. Maybe Evans had
been a little drunk when it started. Whatever, after a considerable time of them
punching, gouging and kicking each other,
Evans had his opponent in a bear hug and
Kolvig, with his arms trapped to his sides,
had tried to reach the knife in his boot. So
Evans had squeezed. Suddenly there was a
small, brittle click, and Kolvig had hung
limp in his arms. Evans realized for the first
time the full extent of his strength: that he'd
broken the other man's back.

The awful thing was, Kolvig didn't die. He
was still alive right now, as far as Evans
knew. A cripple in some poorhouse. He was
a living reminder to Evans of what he was
capable of in anger.

Evans wondered at himself, carrying
around memories of Kolvig as though they
were something he should repent of. He had
no reason to feel guilt! Kolvig had been a
damn dirty foreigner. It had been a fair fight
until he'd tried to stick Evans with a knife.
Evans had been defending himself and what

was wrong with that? And if, sometime soon, he should tangle with Calvin Taylor, (in a fair fight, of course) and the Indian-lover should happen to find himself with his spine snapped too...

CHAPTER FIVE

Taylor might have missed out on supper but next morning the Camerons invited him to breakfast. After eating, he and the major sat drinking Fiona's coffee.

Major Cameron said, 'No water yesterday. How far to the next?'

Taylor clawed at the alkali dust in his trail beard.

'There's tanks that are usually good in Devil's Pass. That cuts through the Superstitions up ahead.'

'You said the Superstitions were Indian country.'

'Apaches are mountain Indians. That's where they like to live, and like to fight.'

'And how far's this ... Devil's Pass?'

'At least thirty mile.'

The two men exchanged grim looks. Cameron was a ghostlike figure, his skin and clothes paled by alkali. But everyone looked like that now, all of them aged by the greying of dust, even the children. Taylor supposed he looked like that too.

Cameron said, 'We won't get there before tomorrow night. I don't know if the stock'll last that long.'

'It'll have to, major.'

There was water in the tanks in Devil's Pass. Not much, and that warm and tasting of alkali, but humans and animals drank gratefully.

Major Cameron damped his bandanna and dabbed at the sunburn on his face. He told Taylor: 'We're more than halfway now!'

Taylor drank from his canteen, rolling the water in his mouth before he swallowed. 'We still got plenty of rough, thirsty country up ahead. Salt flats and such. And no guarantee of any water in it.'

'How far, would you say?'

'To Rio Azul? Fifty miles maybe.'

'Fifty miles?' A day earlier, Cameron thought, the prospect of fifty waterless miles would have been a weight of discouragement crushing him. Now, strangely enough, he felt optimistic. 'Just fifty more miles and we're home.'

Next morning Cameron found there was a new spring in his step as he rose to face the day. From somewhere he seemed to have rediscovered long lost hope. He even waved cheerily at Taylor as the man, mounted on his grey horse, rode out on his first scout. He noted that Fiona watched Taylor riding away.

Cameron's spirits stayed high as he ate his breakfast and moved amongst the travellers. They stayed high even as the day was shaping up to be the hottest yet, and the train crawled eastward between the jaws of grim Devil's Pass. The Superstition Mountains loomed to the north and south, their treeless outlines jagged and hard edged. The travellers made their noon camp, then resumed their journey. After a few miles the caravan inched out of the pass on to an alkali plain.

Cameron mounted his bay horse and rode alongside the wagons. He breathed white dust and felt the power of the midday sun. His eyes began to sting from the glare of the salt flats ahead. But he felt good, except when he remembered Fiona staring after Taylor. Despite his youth, Taylor seemed to be earning his money as a scout. Cameron could imagine how much guts it took to ride out alone ahead of these wagons each day. But what did Cameron really know about him? Did he want his daughter involved with such a man?

Cameron had been riding along in a sort

of reverie; he came out of that suddenly.

There was movement ahead of him. On the eastern skyline.

Cameron shielded his eyes with his hat but it was hard to see. Haze made the horizon fluctuate. Distant mountains beyond the haze flaunted and rippled like something seen through water. He could hear something strange too, a far-off high singing.

Cameron squinted to see into the haze and made out a dark bobbing shape, growing larger. Haze stretched and twisted this shape and then Cameron saw that it was a rider coming towards him. At first he thought it was Taylor, then he saw the man was riding a dark chestnut horse. The point man – Ike Williams – was riding in at the full gallop across the salt flats. He was yelling something.

Ike's galloping horse raised a lot of dust. Behind this pale screen Cameron glimpsed weaving shapes, coming closer. With a dull sense of shock he realized these were horsemen – twenty, thirty of them – boiling up over the horizon with rifles in their hands. They poured out of the haze, on Ike's tail like a pack of wolves.

It came to Cameron that the high singing he'd heard was Apaches yelling. His impressions of them were a blur, flashing images: men in smocks and colourful shirts, their long hair flying bound with rags about their temples. He did register white stripes of war paint barring dark faces.

Ike veered his flagging horse towards the wagons, spurring hard. Behind him rifles cracked.

Ike flopped loosely in the saddle. He seemed to lean sideways and hang there, frozen in the act of toppling. Then he fell, rolling in dust.

The horses of his pursuers ploughed him under. The war party fanned out; they yelled harder as they came at the wagons.

CHAPTER SIX

Calvin Taylor rode in from scouting across the salt flats. A breeze lifted and stirred loose sand, which enveloped him like a shroud. It was a hot, choking, eye-stinging shroud and he pulled his bandanna over his mouth and nose against it. He rode through this dim world, with the sun a gauzy smear behind streaming dust. His mouth twisted at the irony. He was supposed to be a scout, the eyes and ears of the wagon train, and here he was riding blind. A whole tribe of hostiles could be all around him and he wouldn't see them.

After some minutes the wind fell and the dust thinned. Taylor found he could see where he'd been and even where he was going.

He rode, his sore eyes roving over featureless, sun-blasted country. This looked like an endless plain, a flat unbroken surface, but he knew that was deceptive. The plain was torn with breaks and gullies in which considerable numbers of men on foot or horseback might hide. So he rode with his hand close to the Winchester in his saddle sheath and his nerves stretched tight against the bark of a hidden rifle or Apaches rising suddenly like ghosts from the earth.

Occasionally, hard as he tried to keep them focused, his thoughts strayed. Mostly to Fiona Cameron. On the frontier women were married off early, so it was surprising that such a fine-looking woman hadn't caught herself a husband yet. He realized that he knew almost nothing about her. Every time they'd talked it was about him, usually about his supposed love of Indians.

Taylor reined in his horse.

Off to the west there was gunfire.

Taylor's main job was protecting these travellers. The popping of rifles told him he'd failed. *The Apaches had got around him and the wagon train was being attacked.*

He thought of Fiona again, but this time with fear and alarm. He spun his horse. He spurred and the animal broke into a run.

He drove the grey at a full gallop towards the sound of guns.

Taylor rode up a long slope of white sand that came to his horse's knees and plunged through this stuff to the crest. He came in view of the wagon train. The wagons were issuing out of the eastern end of Devil's Pass. A big bunch of Apaches on horseback – perhaps thirty of them – swarmed towards it. There was yelling and gunfire. The lead wagons were turning, circling back into the pass. Dust rose thick as smoke and dim figures afoot and on horseback moved behind it.

Taylor pulled his rifle from his saddle sheath and spurred again. His horse started to move; in the same instant Taylor felt a hard blow against his back that drove him up and forward out of the saddle. He fell, hitting on a mound of loose sand. Dust burst around him. He rolled and scrambled up, knee-deep in fine sand. His horse screamed and reared away. Taylor was utterly confused as to what was happening: had he just been shot in the back? Still he had enough presence of mind left to grab for the trailing lines of the horse as it sprang away. He caught them. The animal danced about.

Taylor bent and snatched up the Winchester and saw two Apaches on horseback galloping towards him, one from the front, one from the right. The latter at least had a rifle, which he pulled to his shoulder and fired. Taylor wasn't hit but his heart jumped in his chest and his arms began to shake with fear. That always happened when he came under fire. He didn't look at the men charging him but concentrated on willing his arms to be still and on holding the reins as the grey tugged at him. 'Hold still, damn you!' The Apaches yelled; one gave the screeching call of a mountain lion. That was designed to panic the horse, he knew. Taylor tried to close his mind to the yelling. He stabbed his foot into the near stirrup and swung aboard the grey as the animal spun beneath him, chasing its tail.

He hauled on the reins brutally, yanking the horse around, making it stand. By which time the Apache charging from the front was almost on him. The Indian drove his pony up the slant. He held a lance, a length of cane with a sliver of metal at the tip. Taylor spurred the grey downslope towards the other man. They yelled. They came together like two old-time knights in storybooks.

The Apache thrust. Taylor swayed and felt the lance pass under his right arm; he swung out with the Winchester in his hand, the barrel catching the Apache across the throat. The pony plunged past, riderless, and the Indian rolled in dust on the slope. Taylor jumped his horse past him as the other Apache veered close, firing from the saddle. Something plucked at Taylor's sleeve. He pulled the Winchester to his shoulder, caught a quick aim on the other's chest and fired.

His shot caught the pony in the head. The animal reared and fell over backwards, spilling the rider. Instantly this man sprang up. He lunged at the oncoming horseman and Taylor kicked him in the chest. The kick lifted the Apache from his feet and flipped him backwards. Taylor swept past, came to the bottom of the slope and reined in there.

As far as he could see, through boiling dust, the wagons were piling back into the pass, teams running flat out. Bringing up the rear, Apaches snapping at its heels, was the Williams's Conestoga. As Taylor had feared, this bulky vehicle was handling badly, swaying perilously as its team ran. Suddenly a wheel went, or jounced over a rock or something and the wagon tilted crazily. He watched in fascinated horror as the wagon overturned. It seemed to happen very slowly, almost gracefully. The Conestoga's covered roof ploughed into earth on its side and dust bloomed over everything. A toppling figure was a dim shape striking the ground and rolling on. It came to its feet and staggered forward out of dust and became Cephas Williams.

Apache horsemen broke from the dust towards him. Cephas began to run. He was running blindly the wrong way, not towards Devil's Pass and the other wagons but towards Calvin Taylor.

Taylor remembered there was a rifle in his hands. As Apaches whipped their ponies in pursuit of the running man, Taylor lifted his Winchester and took aim on them; but before he could fire a bowstring twanged. Cephas staggered, attempted to reach behind him and fell. He made one half-attempt to rise. An arrow stood out between his shoulders, still quivering. Then his strength was gone, he slid forward on to his face.

The riders wheeled their ponies and swarmed around the foundered Conestoga. Dust was thinning, figures emerged from it. Taylor glimpsed Josh Williams swinging his rifle like a club. Horsemen flashed past him. Taylor lifted his rifle and started firing. He hit one rider who pitched sideways. Then he saw Josh had fallen to his knees, his hands gripping the lance in his chest. He toppled.

Taylor heard more yelling, behind him this time. A glance over his shoulder showed Apaches on horseback plunging down the slope towards him.

They were behind him and in front of him. Taylor decided he'd rather take his death in the front than in the back. So he spurred the grey, whacked its rump with his rifle and the animal broke into another run. Towards the wagons.

Apaches were still riding around the capsized Williams vehicle, raising a small dust storm that served to hide him. Suddenly he was amongst them, driving through, crouched low over his horse's withers. He began to hope he could ride right through them unnoticed, hidden by dust and confusion. Then the cry went up: *'Pinda-likoy-ee!'* *'Pinda-likoy-ee!'* ('White eye!' 'White eye!')

Taylor broke from the dust and an Apache swung his pony across his path. On one arm the Indian held a small round shield; in his other hand he lifted a rifle.

Taylor drove the shoulder of his horse into the other man's pony. The pony went down, pinning the rider. The grey staggered but kept its feet and went on running. Taylor was thrown about in the saddle but stayed aboard. Suddenly he was through them.

Apaches were yelling right behind him, almost in his ear; their rifles fired at seemingly point-blank range and yet he wasn't hit. He entered Devil's Pass at full gallop with he didn't know how many Apaches on his heels. A glance over his shoulder showed his pursuers maybe 200 yards back.

The grey started to gasp; its coat was dark with sweat. Foam flew from its mouth and splattered Taylor's legs. But he couldn't afford to be merciful. He used spurs ruthlessly. When he glanced back the next time he'd widened the gap over his pursuers.

He came in view of the wagons fleeing ahead of him. They were driving along the pass at a hard, drumming run. Driving west towards the tanks, where there was still water. And hope, and a place to fort up.

Then he glimpsed movement beyond the wagon train.

A line of horsemen was blocking the pass to the west.

Taylor glimpsed colourful shirts and varicoloured ponies, he heard Apaches yelling as they surged forward. There was a thin crackle of rifle fire.

The lead wagon – he could tell it was the Cameron wagon – veered to the right. Other wagons angled to follow.

Taylor saw why.

There was a break in the wall of mountains on the north side of the pass, the narrow entrance to a canyon. The wagons were turning and disappearing into this canyon.

One wagon couldn't make this right turn. It went over to its left, ploughing into rocks and boulders with a terrible rending crash of splintering wood. There was a high, piercing scream. A woman's scream. Then dust erupted, swallowing the wagon and its occupants, and the first of the oncoming riders streaked through it.

Taylor followed the wagons into the canyon. Apaches followed him. He'd outdistanced the bunch from the east but now he had another pack on his heels. Men on fresher horses.

Once through the canyon entrance the walls peeled back and Taylor was riding into a basin cupped by sheer granite walls. A place of white sand and orange cliffs. The wagons ahead were already on the far side of the basin and circling.

Under him the grey started to cough. Its long, easy stride began to falter. Apaches seemed to be yelling almost in his ear. An arrow whipped by his right shoulder. He risked another backwards glance and saw maybe a dozen Apaches close behind. One man on a paint pony was pulling ahead of his companions, closing on his enemy.

Then there were wagons ahead of Taylor, corralled into a circle and figures moving behind them. There was a dark burst of powder smoke by one wagon, then another. Bullets keened about him. He was caught in a crossfire. *It would be my kind of luck*, he thought, *to be killed by my own side*.

More fire from the wagons; he glanced behind him and saw his pursuers veering away left and right, ducking low on their ponies' necks. All save the man on the paint pony, who kept coming, forgetting all fear in his own battle craziness.

A barricade between wagons was suddenly in front of Taylor. He called on the grey horse one more time and the horse answered. It vaulted the barricade neatly and came down on failing legs.

Taylor glanced back. To his astonishment he saw the Apache plunge his paint pony over the barricade almost on his heels. Before Taylor could react the Apache flung himself from the saddle. He looped his hands around Taylor's neck; both men pitched into the dust between their horses. Taylor half-landed on top of his enemy, which broke his fall.

Both men knelt up. Taylor got his right hand to the knife in his belt sheath, but the Apache was quicker. He swung a stone-headed club and struck Taylor on the left arm, numbing it. In the same instant Taylor drove his knife upwards. The blade went in between the Apache's ribs, all the way to the guard. The Apache gasped; Taylor twisted the knife.

For a second the Apache knelt there, his face full of hatred and pain. Then he was dead and toppling. He fell against Taylor, then past him, and lay on his face in the dust.

Taylor got to his feet. His legs were rubber and shaking, as were his arms. Someone was staring at him in horror. After a time he realized this was Fiona Cameron.

Slowly he came to understand her staring. There was blood all over his shirt although none of it was his. It came from the man he'd knifed.

For the first time he was conscious of a sharp stabbing pain in his back and remembered he might have been shot there. He glanced over his left shoulder and to his alarm saw the tri-feathered shaft of an arrow rising from his back. Taylor grabbed the arrow and found it was caught in the folds of his serape. The wickedly chipped quartz head hadn't even touched his flesh. He turned the missile in his hands, making a small sound of admiration for this simple, deadly thing. Then he dropped it to the earth. Whatever back wound he'd suffered, it couldn't be serious, he was still functioning.

There was gunfire. People in the wagon corral were firing out at Apaches, who swarmed just at the edge of range.

Major Cameron was at the barricade. He took careful aim at a distant enemy, fired and said, 'Missed.' Then he glanced back over his shoulder at Taylor. 'Glad you could join us, Taylor. You might regret it though.'

Taylor felt numb and dizzy and too confused to think. Confused most of all by Cameron's grim humour.

The major said, 'Those Indians are plenty smart. This is a box canyon.' He looked again along the barrel of his rifle. 'They've herded us into a trap here.'

CHAPTER SEVEN

Taylor realized he was in some kind of a daze. But that wouldn't do, he'd have to snap out of it. He'd failed these people once and let them be ambushed. He couldn't afford to fail them again.

He moved over to Cameron. Buck Evans was there too. Evans declared: 'We're out in the open here, major! If we was nearer those bluffs–'

Cameron interrupted him. 'If we were nearer those bluffs Apaches could sniper down on us. Maybe even roll rocks down on us.'

Taylor told Evans, 'At least here you've got a field of fire on all sides.'

'But stuck in the centre of this basin – there's no shade.'

Taylor nodded grimly. 'That's the trade-off. There's no shade.'

Horsemen were dim shapes in the glare of the white plain beyond the wagons. A few of them shouted words he couldn't make out. The occasional rifle cracked.

Taylor turned and looked about him. The wagons were in a loose circle, forming a compound. Mules and oxen had been unyoked and herded into this compound, alongside all the saddle horses that were left. Señora Sanchez sat against a wagon wheel. Her right arm was bloody. Fiona Cameron knelt by her, bandaging her arm, whilst Ramon stood by. A man lay under a wagon, his shirt front all bloody, whilst women crouched by him.

Cameron told Taylor, 'That's Jake Harrison. Hit in the chest.'

Then he's as good as dead, Taylor thought.

There were seven wagons. Taylor asked: 'Who did we lose, Major?'

'The Williams. Three of 'em anyway. The Veidts. Their wagon overturned getting into this canyon. And the McShanes.'

Evans worked moisture in his jaw, not finding enough to spit. 'I saw that. They got poor old McShane right off. Shot one of his mules so he couldn't move, then they was all over his wagon. I heard his kids ... screaming.'

Cameron's face was bleak. 'All the wagons with children.' He swallowed. 'I led all those young, innocent people to their deaths.'

Señora Sanchez lifted her anguished face

towards them. 'All those poor children.'

Taylor said, 'They might not be dead. Apaches don't kill kids normally, mostly they keep 'em to raise.'

Evans lifted an eyebrow. 'Raise?'

'As Apaches.'

'That's worse than being dead.'

'No it isn't. Sometimes they spare women too, to keep as slaves.' He doubted that was Frau Veidt's fate; he remembered the terrible smashing impact as the Veidt wagon overturned, a woman's high, nerve-shredding scream...

Señora Sanchez looked at him beseechingly. 'But Mr Veidt... Mr McShane...'

Taylor didn't answer and Señora Sanchez began to wail. Other women joined in. They made a fiendish high keening, an inhuman sound. And yet, Taylor supposed, it was the most human of sounds.

Taylor did a quick inventory of what was left, people, stock, supplies, food and water, weapons and ammunition. They were down five men, two women and eight children. Twenty-two remained: eight women and fourteen men, including Taylor, Ramon Sanchez and Jake Harrison, lying under his wagon with a fist-sized hole in his chest. Taylor took a look at his own back injury and found an angry red bullet crease that had bled plenty but was still only a graze. He also saw to his horse.

Then he rejoined Cameron and Evans at their barricade.

Evans said, 'What I don't figure is – why didn't they just swarm all over us? They'd've finished us easy. There was a big bunch on our tails, then most of 'em broke off. Why?' He glared at Taylor. 'Well, Mister Indian scout?'

'When Apaches go raiding, it's mostly for plunder. So those three wagons we lost bought the rest of us time. Lots of Apaches went after them, to see what they could loot.' He started to build a cigarette with fingers that only trembled slightly. 'And they seem low on modern weapons. Bows and arrows, old muskets, but not many repeaters. If they'd been well-armed none of us would have made it into this canyon.'

Evans scowled. 'Our situation's still pitiful. There must be sixty, seventy of them at least. We've got what – fourteen men? No, thirteen, if you take out poor old Harrison there. Twelve you take out that 'breed kid. We can't even make a proper wagon circle. They could wipe us out in one charge.'

Taylor lit his cigarette. 'But they'd lose

men doing it. Apaches are guerrilla fighters. They don't take heavy casualties if they can help it.'

'A coward's way to fight.'

'Maybe. Some might say they're being smart.'

Evans mouth twisted with anger. 'You got to defend them, don't you? Even after this. Even after what they done to the Williamses, and McShane—'

Cameron made an impatient sound. 'We can argue this another time. Point is, Taylor, you don't think they'll try a straight attack?'

'Unlikely. Why should they? They'll just let the sun work on us through tomorrow. That way they get what they're after – our guns and ammunition and supplies – intact.'

'You figure they'll just hunker down to a siege? I didn't think Indians had that kind of patience.'

'Major, they don't know what time is. So they're not always running against it.'

Cameron wiped sweat from his face with his hand. 'We're not finished yet. In half an hour the sun'll be down. And it's lucky we filled up with water this morning. That should hold us a couple days, we spread it between us and the stock.'

Taylor thought of his grey horse, standing

trembling, fear, pain and bewilderment in its eyes. How brutally he'd used the animal today. How he'd nearly ridden it to death. That put an edge of temper in his voice. 'The hell with the stock! We don't know how long we could be penned in here. We need the water, not them.'

'Without water the animals'll die. That's damn cruel–'

Taylor let his temper rip. 'This is cruel country, Major. I warned you! I told you it was crazy to make this trip, but hell no, you wouldn't listen! You had to find your paradise.'

Cameron's face flushed with anger but it was Evans who answered. 'You're a big talker, Taylor! The great Indian scout! It was your job to stop us getting ambushed! So how come the Indians got round you?'

Taylor started to reply, then decided he didn't have an answer to that.

Evans glared some more. After a time he stalked off.

Taylor and Cameron stood in awkward silence. Eventually Cameron said, 'So – what can we do? Are there military in this neighbourhood?'

'Soldiers are pretty thin on the ground out here. There's the Morrison ranch maybe fifty miles north. Big spread. They're a tough outfit. They have to be, ranching in Apache country. If we could get a rider to them...'

'Apaches'll have the mouth of the canyon all stoppered up. Think anyone can get through?'

'We can try.'

Cameron thought a moment. He nodded. 'Tonight then. I suggest the boy, Ramon. He can ride, he's light in the saddle. More to the point,' he added grimly, 'he's the youngest of us.'

Ramon Sanchez asked, 'What are you doing?'

Taylor crouched down at the feet of Ramon's roan horse. He said, 'Chiricahua Apache trick. They shoe their horses in deerskin boots – which I've got a spare pair of, here. Muffles sound.'

Taylor stood. His Hamilton watch told him it was just gone 10 p.m. There was an amber, nearly full moon but no stars, which meant the night around them was dark enough: deep blue-black sky above sable-black canyon walls. He told Ramon: 'You want to lead your horse until you're in the mouth of the canyon. Walk right through 'em.'

Major Cameron said, 'Once you're there,

mount up and ride like hell. Understand? We're all depending on you, Ramon!'

Ramon swallowed, his fear clearly showing. 'When do I start?'

Taylor said, 'Soon as you hear guns.'

'Guns?'

'We're going to create a diversion. Up the other end of the canyon. Skirmish 'em a little.'

'You're going out there? You're crazy!'

Taylor smiled grimly. 'No doubt about that.' He reached out and shook the boy's hand. 'Good luck, Ramon.'

Taylor's smile, the optimism he put into his voice, told a lie. There was a cold weight of dread in his belly, the near-certainty that this boy was going to his death...

Taylor's skirmishers slithered out of the wagon compound on their bellies, snaking along for a few hundred yards. Taylor's shot was their signal to fire away at nothing, as if they had a limitless supply of ammunition. A few minutes of that and they began to draw return fire. At which point Taylor yelled for them to fall back. They all made it back to the wagons without injury.

Cameron said, 'You kicked up a good diversion, Taylor. Ramon managed to sneak out. I think maybe he made it.'

'Let's hope so.'

Taylor walked to the edge of the compound and gazed out. It was a cold night and he had forbidden fires (which gave light for snipers to shoot into the camp) so most of the party huddled miserably in their wagons under extra layers of blankets. Taylor, who hated cold, pulled his serape tighter about him and flexed his chilled fingers on the grip of his rifle.

He turned at a soft footfall. Fiona Cameron approached. She asked, 'Are you all right?'

He nodded. 'How're you doing?'

'I'm like my father.' A trace of a smile showed on her lips. 'I'm tough.'

'I guess you are.'

She surprised him then; she reached out and touched his arm.

Before he could react to that she turned and walked away. Taylor stared after her, not for the first time mystified by the doings of women. And he'd thought she was Buck Evans's girl!

Thinking of her hand on his arm, a smile worked at his lips, just about the first smile he'd managed today. Then, a coyote yarred in the dark beyond the wagons. Coyote or

Apache? That hair-raising keening snatched away pleasant thoughts and reminded him of where he was.

He was grateful she hadn't asked him, just now, what their chances were. He didn't think he could lie to her. His every instinct told him this was a dead man's hand, that the Apaches held all the cards and there was no way out. He doubted Ramon could make it through to the Morrison ranch, or this wagon party could fight off even one serious attack. If the Indians decided to shoot fire arrows into these wagons, for example, they could wipe out the Cameron party in minutes. He supposed the only reason they didn't do that was because they wanted the wagons and material intact. So the migrants survived only on Apache sufferance.

And if they were overrun, what would happen to Fiona Cameron? She might be killed. Or they might spare her. She'd be raped, of course, then dragged off to a life as little more than a pack animal in some mountain rancheria. Or maybe they'd take her to Mexico and sell her into slavery.

It had been quiet as dusk fell, although Taylor had heard distant music and singing at the mouth of the canyon. He guessed the Apaches had been celebrating their partial victory with a sing and maybe a feast. Now he glimpsed pitch-pine torches glimmering and moving in the darkness on the cliffs above, as Apaches climbed up there. The Indians were clearly in no hurry about finishing the job they'd started. Meanwhile they slowly tightened the noose around the wagons...

CHAPTER EIGHT

Before first light the next morning Taylor stood at the barricade, his Winchester laid across his arm. He got the other men on first watch up too, amongst them the Evans brothers. They came cursing and grumbling from their blankets.

Taylor didn't expect the Mescaleros would attack yet. More likely they'd let the sun work on the white eyes today and then swarm all over the wagons at first light tomorrow. But you couldn't lay down rules when it came to Apaches and dawn was always the most dangerous time, their favoured time of attack.

In the dark beyond the wagons a coyote yipped and a turkey gobbled. Taylor smiled bitterly. Apaches could normally impersonate these creatures so well they'd fool turkeys and coyotes. But this morning they weren't trying. They couldn't hide the mockery and contempt in their voices.

Cameron came and joined Taylor. He thrust a cup of coffee into the younger man's hand.

Taylor said, 'Well, I've got your people into a fine state of affairs here.'

'You can't blame yourself for all this.'

'Yes I can, Major. If I was hired for one reason, it was to make sure hostiles didn't jump us.'

'I don't know much about Apaches, but from what I hear, they've ambushed the smartest men who ever lived.'

Taylor didn't want to argue. He stared out at the paling darkness.

The men at the barricades waited. Full light came, and no attack.

Taylor scanned the surrounding country with his field glasses. A few Apaches showed, on foot and on horseback, but they were out of range.

He felt tension ease out of him in a long sigh. He told the men at the barricades: 'All right. Normal guard rota. Rest of you can stand down. Go back to bed if you want.'

'What?' Buck Evans gave him a surprised look. 'That's your plan? Just sit here, do nothing?'

'Doing nothing's usually the best bet, 'specially when it gets hot. More you move, more you sweat, more water you need.'

The people in the corral ate their breakfasts and then lay in their wagons, or under them, or in what shade they could find. The sun climbed in a bleached-out sky. The livestock made the pitiful sounds of thirsty animals. The farmyard stink of their droppings and voiding lay over the wagon corral like a thick blanket. Humming flies swarmed. Occasionally Jake Harrison moaned, or talked in delirium. Apart from that there was almost no talking in the compound. Taylor missed Josh Williams's mouth organ.

Around noon Cameron said, 'Something's happening.'

Taylor strode over to the barricade, where men were gathered with rifles in their hands. He stood between Davy Harrison (Jake's son) and the Evans brothers and gazed out. The noon sun made a haze that swayed and distorted the plain before him. Then the haze moved and Taylor saw a body of horsemen. They were at the edge of range, maybe 700 yards.

Taylor trained his field glasses on the distant horsemen. After a moment of study he told the others: 'See the big fellow in the red shirt, on the white horse? That's Loco.'

Buck Evans sucked on a pebble. Around that he said, 'Wish I had my buffalo gun. Sold it to help buy my wagon.' His mouth twisted with bitterness. 'If I still had that old Sharps, I'd make *El Jefe* out there jump.'

Davy Harrison said, 'You can't hit a man at that range.' Harrison wasn't more than thirty, but his hair, moustache and thin fringe of beard were prematurely grey. His face was old and gloomy before its time. That had been the case even before the Apaches attacked and his father took what was maybe a mortal wound.

Buck said, 'You never hear about the Adobe Walls fight? One buffalo hunter hit an Indian at more'n fifteen hundred yards there.'

Cameron asked Taylor, 'You think they're going to rush us?'

Taylor put his field glasses on the horsemen once more. Suddenly a man on a paint pony pushed his mount forward. He held a long rope which he jerked. A man afoot staggered along behind him. This man was held by the rope tied around his wrists.

There was an icy coldness in Taylor's belly that seemed to spread through him slowly. Some of what he felt must have shown in his face, because Cameron asked: 'What is it?'

Taylor passed him the field gasses. It was a minute before Cameron saw and then he said, in a bare whisper: 'Ramon Sanchez.'

Cameron lowered the field glasses and returned them to Taylor. The Scot looked defeated, an old and broken man.

Ramon was naked but for his white cotton pants. There might be blood on his face and on his feet. He called out in a cracked, thirsty voice that carried clearly to the wagons: 'Help me, Major! Taylor!'

Cameron asked, 'What are they trying to do, set up a trade?'

'What have we got to trade? They're just taunting us, and playing with him.'

A warrior jabbed Ramon with his lance and the prisoner stumbled forward. He called plaintively: 'Please, somebody! Help me! Taylor!' Apaches laughed and jeered.

Taylor heard a high wailing cry behind him. He turned. Señora Sanchez was clambering on to the barricade. Fiona Cameron ran towards her. Fiona grabbed the older woman's arm but she squirmed free and sprang to earth beyond, running out into the desert. She cried: 'Ramon! Ramon!'

Fiona Cameron plunged over the barricade after her. Major Cameron and Harrison ran out after Fiona. Calvin Taylor ran after them.

Señora Sanchez ran ten yards before her skirt tripped her. Cameron and Harrison caught her. The woman screamed and kicked and fought against them. They had to half-carry and half-drag her back towards the wagons. Taylor moved beyond them, covering their retreat with his rifle.

Movement rippled through the horsemen, there was yelling and jeering but no surge towards the wagons. One Apache, afoot, strode forward. He turned his back, threw up the flap of his breechclout and slapped his bare rump.

Taylor felt cold anger. He pulled his rifle to his shoulder. The Apache was out of range but Taylor didn't care. He took a shot at him anyway. The man laughed derisively. Another Apache called out in English: 'Hey, Shadow Man, we can see you! You're dead!' As Taylor returned to the wagons, he was followed by the taunting cries of coyote and turkey.

Señora Sanchez sat against a wagon wheel with a huddle of women about her. Fiona Cameron had her arms about the older woman; she made soothing noises, as if to a child. Señora Sanchez began to call Ramon's name, over and over.

Buck Evans leaned on the barricade. 'What was it that Indian called you, Taylor? Shadow Man? What's that mean?'

'Hard to explain. A shadow ain't just a shadow to an Indian.'

Taylor lifted his field glasses and did some more scanning. Something kept pulling his attention to a towering bluff, red as a wound, off to the east.

There was movement and Taylor trained his field glasses on it.

Ramon's captor had become restless. He mounted his pony and walked it up and down. Ramon was pulled to his feet and staggered behind, on the end of the rope. He went to his knees and was half-dragged, then pulled to his feet again.

Cameron asked Taylor: 'What's happening?'

Taylor studied the man on the paint pony, sensing his impatience. The man flicked the quirt in his hand, as if he was eager to run his horse...

It occurred to Taylor that Señora Sanchez had fallen silent. Now she stood and gazed out over the barricade. Suddenly she called her son's name.

Maybe Ramon heard. He gave a great, wailing cry of despair. He lunged forward, as if he thought he might escape. The man on the paint pony reared his horse, yanking on the rope and jerked Ramon off his feet.

Ramon rose dazedly, only to be jerked off his feet again. This happened a couple more times and Apaches laughed.

As Ramon rose wearily once more, his captor gave a high wild cry. He heeled the flanks of his paint pony and the pony started running. Ramon ran behind it, hauled along by the rope, and his captor veered his pony across a scatter of loose stones and broken rocks. Ramon began to scream as the stones and rocks lacerated his bare feet. He fell and was dragged in a trail of dust. The Apache reined in his paint.

Very slowly his captive rose. Ramon was a ghost, white with dust all over, including his pants, and then blood started to show through and covered his chest, legs and face. He staggered drunkenly. The Apache yelled again and kicked his horse in the ribs once more. He raced his horse in a wide circle. Ramon fell and was dragged. The Apache dragged him across the bed of stones and rocks and out of them and round and back across the stony bed a second time, and then a third.

Señora Sanchez cried her son's name. The cry became a terrible, rending scream. It ended on a piercing note that seemed beyond the limits of a human voice. Then she seemed to faint, slumping in Fiona Cameron's arms, and the younger woman lowered her to the earth.

There was a silence of horror in the wagon compound.

It was ended by Buck Evans. He asked Taylor: 'Why don't you tell us what human beings Apaches are? About their sense of humour?'

Taylor sat with his back to the barricade, clenching and unclenching his hands around the barrel of his Winchester. He heard Señora Sanchez's scream in his head. It went into his teeth and into his brain and echoed again and again in his ears.

Afternoon heat and blinding light fell on the wagon compound. People retreated into shrinking amounts of shade. Flies tormented thirsty livestock. A horse fell and died. There was barely a word spoken. And then Señora Sanchez started crying out Ramon's name.

Next, one of the older women, Mrs Kruger, raised her voice. She had a harsh, whining voice at the best of times, and now, cracked with thirst, it was a rusty, grating instrument. She called on the Lord to smite the Amalekites.

Ethan Evans told her, 'I don't see no

Amalekites out there, Ma, only Apaches!' but she ignored him. She told the Apaches: '*As your sword made women childless, so shall your mother be made childless amongst women...*'

Taylor's own father had fancied himself as a preacher, especially when he was in his cups – which was often – particularly keen on quoting the wrathful and vengeful passages of the Old Testament. So Taylor had heard a lot about the smiting of Amalekites (and others). He could almost hear his father's voice as she declared: '*Therefore go and strike Amalek and devote to destruction all that they have... Do not spare them, but kill both man and woman, child and infant, ox and sheep, camel and donkey...*'

Ethan Evans had been shading up under his wagon. He rolled out from under it now and stood. He told Mrs Kruger: 'Don't be calling on God, you crazy old woman! There ain't none! There ain't no heaven, and there ain't no hell!'

Buck stirred in the shade where he lay. 'Oh yes there is. There's hell all right. Where do you think we are, right now?'

CHAPTER NINE

Taylor thought: *you're right there, Buck.*

This was hell's half-acre all right. Except it was less than half an acre.

One reason Taylor had come West was to find freedom in limitless space and endless distance. Only now his world was little more than a few dozen yards across in any direction, hemmed in by walls of canvas and wood. The space thus enclosed was filled with suffering humans and animals dying of thirst, being driven crazy by a myriad flies. The air he breathed was choking and foul. In the background, suitable to this madhouse, a crazed woman droned on about destruction and revenge.

Ethan Evans moved back into shade. In a half-whisper that Taylor heard he told his brother, 'Listen to that old loon. That's what happens when you get religion.'

Taylor came to a decision. He took his hands from his rifle and found they ached from gripping the barrel so tightly. He stood and used his field glasses to study the bluffs once more. Then he went on a little quest about the wagons. Next he approached Cameron.

The Scot sat in a small piece of shade by his wagon. He'd damped his bandanna and draped it over his face. Fiona lay under the wagon, holding Señora Sanchez. Both women seemed to be asleep. Cameron told Taylor: 'This is like being in Dante's *Inferno*. God's mercy there's no children amongst us.'

'Major, can I speak to you?'

They moved to the far side of the compound, out of earshot of the others. Taylor said, 'I checked – we've got plenty of rope.'

'What?'

'I was looking at that bluff off east. The deep red one. Up on the west side there's a sort of a zigzagging trail. I think a party can climb up there.'

'You're crazy! Those bluffs are sheer!'

'No, they're not.'

Cameron fanned flies away from his face with his hat. 'Sun's got to you Taylor. You're as cracked as poor Mrs Kruger.'

'Major, listen to me. Nobody knows what Apaches'll do. More'n'likely though, they're going to hit us at dawn tomorrow. No need for 'em to wait any longer. When that happens, we can't hold 'em. You agree? We'll all die – slow or quick – unless they carry off some of the women as slaves. So our only chance is to climb that bluff tonight.'

Cameron thought about it. 'Only needs a couple of Apaches on top of the bluff to pick us off one by one.'

'Sure. That might happen. But my guess is most of 'em'll be gathered at the mouth of the canyon, ready to charge in. So we create another diversion. Take some men down there and attack *them* first. Whilst that's going on, the rest of us climb the bluff and out of this trap.'

'Attack them? How many men would attack them?'

'I figure four.'

'Another crazy plan! Four men attack the whole bunch? How much chance would they have?'

Taylor swallowed against the dryness in his throat. 'None. They'd be dead men. But they might keep the Indians occupied long enough for the rest of us to escape.'

'You'd ask four men to sacrifice their lives? While you climbed out of here?'

'No. *You* take the people up the bluff, Major. I'd be down the canyon. With three volunteers to side me when we hit them.'

Cameron glared at him. 'What is this? Your way of atoning, because you feel guilty you let us get ambushed? I told you, it wasn't your fault. Apaches have jumped smarter men than you.'

'If I'm going to send men to their deaths, least I can do is keep 'em company.'

Cameron shook his head dismissively.

Anger came into Taylor's voice. 'At least if we try this, we have a chance. We sit and wait here, there's no chance.'

'Crazy!'

'All right, Major, you tell me: what else can we do?'

As dusk fell Taylor found one private place in this enclosure packed with humans and animals. That was the Sanchez wagon. Señora Sanchez slept right now by the Cameron wagon so Taylor had taken her space in order to get the last sleep he'd ever enjoy.

Major Cameron had agreed to his plan as Taylor knew he would; there was no alternative. Taylor paused in the shadows behind the Sanchez wagon. He would snatch a few hours' sleep in poor Ramon's bed and then lead his diversion party into the canyon.

He remembered Nachay's safe-passage belt, still in his saddle-bags. That might save him if the Apaches took him alive, though he doubted it. He'd been prominent in fighting the Mescaleros and had killed a few of them. That would count against whatever value a strip of dried pony skin might otherwise have. No, better to accept his fate as certain. He just hoped the end was quick. It was curious how calm he felt about this business, now that a decision had been made.

Taylor pulled open the back flap of the wagon; then something moved in the shadows near him. His hand went instinctively to the Colt pistol in his cross-draw holster before he saw who it was, then he moved his hand from the gun.

She said, 'My father told me what we're going to do. What *you're* going to do.'

'I need to sleep, Fiona. There's no time to talk.'

She came close to him. 'No, there isn't.'

He opened his mouth to reply and she placed her fingertips over his lips. She took his hand and led him towards the wagon.

A man about to die, Taylor thought, ought not to feel this good. But feel good he did. He was trying not to grin like a damn fool as his little band of heroes gathered about him.

It was just gone midnight. There was a full moon and no stars on ink-black darkness. The air was chill. Matt Williams was there, and Davy Harrison. Then the third man came towards them.

Taylor was surprised. 'Ethan.'

Evans smiled sardonically. 'What's the matter, Taylor, don't you want me?'

'I didn't expect you.'

'Buck and I tossed for it. He won.'

These men blackened their hands and faces with boot polish and black ash from a dead fire. They checked and oiled their rifles with silent, grim care. Taylor pulled on a pair of knee-length Apache moccasins, grass stuffed into the soles to muffle sound. Matt Williams started blackening the blade of a long stabbing knife, something like an 'Arkansas toothpick'. Taylor asked him, 'Who you fixing to stick with that?'

'I smell out a scalp, I figure I'll take it. Get one of theirs before they get mine.'

Harrison said, 'I heard Apaches don't take white men's scalps. That right, Taylor? Only Mexicans, cus they pay bounty on Apache hair.'

Ethan said, 'Maybe Mr Taylor here don't approve of scalping Indians.'

Williams glared at Taylor. 'It ain't your

three brothers dead out there.'

Harrison nodded, maybe thinking of his father: Jake Harrison had died a few hours back. Taylor might feel touched that these men had opted to die with him, but he knew their main motivation was revenge.

He said, 'That's something. You *can* smell them. They rub themselves with bear grease.'

Cameron came from the darkness, shook their hands and wished them luck. He stared at Taylor, then nodded, for no reason Taylor could understand. The Scot faded into the dark.

The four remaining men stood in awkward silence. Taylor got his thoughts back from Fiona Cameron. He'd already said his goodbyes to her. He asked the men with him, 'Ready?' They gave grunts of assent. He thought he ought to say something and waited for the words to come. After fifteen seconds of that, Ethan said, 'Let's get on with it, for Christ's sake!'

CHAPTER TEN

The four men got down on their faces and crawled on their bellies away from the wagons.

As the jaws of the canyon loomed before and around him, Taylor came to rocks. He slid into the cover they provided gratefully. Crossing open ground, snaking along naked of cover in the eye of the moon, had shredded his nerves. The strange calm he'd felt earlier was gone. Now fear was dry in his throat and his arms trembled. Despite the chill of the night his face was damp with sweat.

He lay between rocks and waited for the others.

For a moment he thought about Fiona Cameron. Remembering the brief time they'd had he could feel warm pleasure, and then bitter resentment. To find a woman like that and then lose her almost immediately! Maybe to lose her to Buck Evans after all!

A whisper of sound; then Evans, Williams and Harrison crouched around him.

Harrison was attempting a smile, although fear made it something off-kilter and grotesque. The others stared at Taylor grimly.

They'd decided their plan earlier, such plan as it was. Head up the canyon. As soon as one of them came in sight of an Apache (or thought he did) he'd open fire and the others would back him up. They'd raise as much hell and kill as many Indians as they could before the end came. And hope they weren't taken alive...

As Taylor studied these men's faces for what he knew was the last time his throat was dry. He nodded and they moved off. Then he was alone. He supposed just about as alone as he'd ever been.

He followed the others into the black gut of the canyon. He tried to ignore the fear that hummed through him and smelled faintly on his skin like sulphur.

He tried to move almost silently but every small noise he made seemed to crash violently, to fill the night, rattling like a coin in a tin cup.

He paused once more, stretching out on his belly.

He strained to see and identified blotches of paler darkness in the gloom. A scatter of small boulders. Boulders or blankets with

Apaches huddled under them? He listened to the thick, throbbing silence around him. He could see or hear nothing yet his nerves quivered with the feeling of enemies all around him, closing in...

There was sudden movement in the darkness; a man broke from it, running towards him.

Taylor lifted his rifle, glimpsing the pale hair and beard of Davy Harrison.

Harrison got halfway to him, grunted and stumbled. He went down on all fours. He groped around on the earth, an arrow angling up from the back of his neck. Another shape broke from the dark behind him: a man running forward, swinging the club in his hand.

Taylor fired.

The charging man kept running, on legs that suddenly had no strength. He plunged headlong, struck the earth on one shoulder and rolled.

Taylor started to rise. Suddenly there was a pungent odour in his nose – bear grease!

He turned his head. The black silhouette of a man loomed above him, thrusting down with the lance in his hands. He cried the Apache word *'Zas-tee!'* – 'Kill!'

Taylor dodged the lance, driving his head

into the Apache's stomach. The man grunted, doubled forward and pitched headlong over his enemy. Taylor stood and something like a strong wire caught him across the throat, jerking him backwards. He fell; other figures reared out of the dark about him. Taylor lifted his rifle and took a blow on his right arm, which numbed it. He let the rifle fall. He felt terror then and tried to squirm off the earth. He could tell someone had hooked a bow over his head, the bowstring was burning into the flesh of his throat. He heard gunfire and yelling, and he heard, too, the gagging sounds he made.

Taylor struggled to his knees. An Apache stood over him, swinging the rifle in his hands across his body. Taylor tried to dodge the rifle butt as it arced towards him. He was too slow. Pain exploded against his right temple and bright colours flashed. Then he was lying on his back on the earth and the night sky above him reeled and toppled, a black wall falling towards him. The bone-white moon fell too, shot out of the sky, and in falling turned black.

The moon wasn't dead but rode the starless sky above. Taylor watched it out of one eye, because his right eye was closed, glued down by the dried blood on the right-hand side of his face. Pain roared and throbbed in his head. He registered pain in his wrists also. He discovered his wrists and ankles were tied tightly by some kind of hair rope. He lay on a slight slope, head pointing up-hill. He was stretched out like an X on the cold, hard ground, the ropes tied to posts hammered into the earth.

If he wasn't cold enough from the night what he saw was enough to freeze his blood. Apaches stood around him. Perhaps half a dozen men. The chevrons of white bottom-clay that split their faces made them seem like a gathering of fierce, dark hawks. They all had weapons in their hands.

This was the worst nightmare of any white man on the frontier: to be taken for torture by hostile Indians. He ought to be shaking with fear. When he came out of his present dazed state he'd be plenty afraid, he supposed. Right now all he felt was a dizzy sense of unreality, and the pain in his head.

Taylor wasn't sure where he was, perhaps on the flats east of Devil's Pass. The night sky looked to be at its darkest, dawn one or two hours off. His nose caught the acrid stink of recent burning, maybe a small fire just gone out, a faint smell of roasting meat... In nearby shadows, a man whimpered in pain. He lifted his voice and cried: 'God help me!'

Taylor tried to clear his head of its hurting and confusion long enough to identify the voice. Before he could an Apache stepped forward and stared down at him.

It was Loco.

Taylor wondered if Nachay was with this bunch. Loco's son might have died of his wound in the desert, after Taylor found him there, but the white man doubted it. As a rule Apaches were hard to kill.

Loco was taller than the men with him, though stocky and barrel-chested as most of them were. He was wearing his trademark red shirt. Loco was in his fifties, Taylor supposed, his chest-length hair almost purely grey. Taylor expected him to glare at the prisoner in hatred and anger. Instead his face showed something like sadness. He looked a tired man, full of his years. Strangely Taylor was reminded, for a moment, of Major Cameron.

Loco turned away abruptly. Someone was approaching. Taylor heard a new sound, one that didn't belong in an Apache camp. The Apaches' deerskin moccasins made little sound on the earth, but this newcomer's footfall made a noisy crunching over loose stones and gravel. *Whoever it was wore boots.*

Taylor lifted his head and strained to see, but the newcomer was above and behind him.

Loco and the other Apaches turned their backs on Taylor. They walked upslope towards the newcomer, out of Taylor's view. Voices came. Taylor strained to hear. After a moment he determined the talk was in Spanish, the universal language of the South-west. He heard Loco say: 'You're only just in time. Have you got the rifles?'

A man replied: 'Have you got the money, *jefe?*'

There was some more talk, which Taylor missed, then voices faded out.

All sound faded out, leaving pristine silence. Taylor waited for the Apaches to return. They didn't.

He decided that, inexplicably, he'd been left alone here. He started to pull at his ropes. Then there was a small rushing sound, boots churning loose stones, and a little music after that.

Taylor held still, listening. Slowly he turned his head. All he saw was the darkness of the slope above him and to his right. Gradually he made out a column of thicker darkness on the night: a man standing there.

He was entirely in shadow and then he moved forward a few steps. Taylor heard his boots again and a small, bell-like ringing.

He knew what that was: the man had jingle-bobs, tiny pear-shaped pendants hanging from the ends of the spur rowels on his boots. They made a slight, pretty music.

Taylor felt the man's eyes on him and waited for him to move closer. Instead he heard the faint sounds of boots and spurs retreating upslope. They lost themselves in distance. After a time Taylor decided he was alone again.

He thought about the man with jingle-bobs on his spurs. Taylor hadn't been able to place an accent, but the gunrunner was undoubtedly an American.

Taylor remembered something he'd said to somebody – Cameron perhaps – something like: *If they'd been well-armed, none of us would have made it into this canyon.*

The Apaches might be just about to get themselves well-armed. And if they caught the Cameron party scaling the bluff, in no position to fight... A scene played in Taylor's mind's eye, he heard people screaming as they died, he heard Fiona Cameron's scream...

He strained at his tethering ropes, bring-sing blood at his wrists, to no avail. Then he lay, defeated, and watched the sky turn grey-black as false dawn came.

He'd forgotten the man nearby, who started moaning again, asking God in Heaven to help him. Taylor could now identify this man from what remained of his voice. It seemed Ethan Evans had found religion at last.

CHAPTER ELEVEN

Taylor tried again at his ropes but only succeeded in bringing more blood to his wrists. And more pain to his head.

Ethan Evans made small, pitiful sounds that showed he was still –just – alive.

Pain was like an axe blade that someone had used to split Taylor's skull and then left in there. After some indeterminate time it eased a little – though not much – and he could think. And remember. The fight in the canyon. Putting the pieces of his memories together, Taylor at last realized what had happened. They'd been ambushed. *Loco had been waiting for them.*

Taylor had told Nachay: 'Your daddy's pretty smart.' He hadn't known the half of it. Loco had out-thought and out-guessed his enemies at every turn, from the first ambush through to the fiasco in the canyon. Taylor wondered if he was maybe the smartest Apache leader since Cochise. If he'd had a thousand warriors in his band, instead of a hundred or less, he might have been able to hold off the white eyes for years. But it was too late for that now, and maybe Loco knew it. All he could do was slow down the final advance of the invaders, wound and harass them, until he was, himself, hunted down.

Taylor heard, distantly, gunfire.

There was a lot of it, and it came fast: rapid-firing weapons.

Taylor listened in fear and horror. If the Apaches had caught the Cameron party scaling the bluffs, what chance would they have? What chance would Fiona have?

There was a small sound in the darkness by his right ear, the rasp of a moccasin against the earth. A shape loomed over him. Taylor couldn't see the face clearly but glimpsed a stripe of white-bottom-clay banding the cheeks. He felt a sudden fear, but that became bewilderment as he saw the Apache crouch down and pull at the stake-pin by Taylor's right wrist. When the Indian got the pin fairly loose he reached towards the prisoner. He placed something in Taylor's right hand: it was a knife with a bone haft.

Nachay said, 'Better go quick, Shadow Man.'

Then he was gone.

Taylor lay still a moment, trying to sort out the confusion in his thoughts. Then he started yanking at the loosened stake pin. He worked it free and used the knife to cut his remaining bonds.

Whilst he did he heard a change in the distant firing. It eased considerably, slackening to short sporadic bursts. Which meant either the wagon people had got away, or they were all dead.

Taylor attacked his bonds with renewed urgency. The loosening of the ropes brought exquisite pain to his wrists and ankles, and sitting up drove an iron spike through his skull. But he couldn't think about that, with what might be happening in Devil's Pass. He staggered to his feet.

Dawn was pushing up over the eastern mountains and turning the land and sky pink. It showed him Ethan Evans. Evans was thirty yards away. He was naked and sitting up, tied to a stubby barrel-head cactus so the long spines drove into his back. A piece of dampened rawhide had been tied around his temples, to crush his skull as it contracted. His legs were splayed and a small fire had been built on his belly and his crotch, though it was dead now, a pile of white ash.

Taylor had seen things and had a strong stomach but he might have vomited at this ghastly sight, except he had nothing in his stomach to bring up. Ethan had still been alive only a short while ago, which seemed incredible, but now he was a nodding corpse.

Taylor supposed he'd been lucky on a couple of counts. Normally novice warriors, boys about fourteen, would have been left behind to guard prisoners but maybe Loco had taken only seasoned warriors with him on this raid; and Taylor had been taken unconscious, so spared Ethan's fate, at least to begin with.

Taylor turned away from the dead man. He moved towards the sound of gunfire. And then it came to him: there was no gunfire...

He entered the eastern end of Devil's Pass, where the MacShane wagon lay, and the Williams's Conestoga. He found no bodies. He guessed the Apaches had dragged off the dead white eyes, rather than leave corpses to bloat and stink in the canyon mouth. Taylor kept to the cover of rocks along the canyon wall. He heard the drumming of hoofs and hid inside a circle of small boulders, but the sound receded, the horsemen moving away from him.

Taylor's head was full of gnawing pain and some of the heat haze of the desert seemed to have found its way on to his head, so he seemed to be moving through a blinding sun-yellow dream, in which nothing seemed real, and he was too numb to feel anything. He'd seen what the Apaches had done to Ethan Evans and felt nothing. Now he stood over Davy Harrison: the man lay dead at his feet and that didn't seem real either. Harrison had his hands to the back of his neck, to the arrow embedded there, his mouth was wide open and screaming, the face frozen in its final pain. Matt Williams lay nearby. Both men had been stripped naked, but showed only a few random mutilations, presumably inflicted after they were dead. Neither was scalped. Harrison had been right about that.

Taylor came to the mouth of the canyon. The earth near him was churned by many hoofs and to the west a haze of fine dust was slowly settling. There was an eerie quiet as he went into the canyon, then he heard a strange snapping and crackling. And smelled smoke.

In the basin the wagons were still burning. A lifting wind drove a screen of grey smoke across. It brought tears to his eyes and he coughed over it. All the livestock had been driven off, including his grey horse. He skirted the blackened hulks of wood and canvas being licked by small flames and walked towards distant bluffs. He'd lost track of time because it had been dawn and now the sun was high towards noon. It burned his flesh and laid a fiery hand on the pounding in his head. It scoured his eyeballs and turned the world to white light, a dazzling mist that he found he was staggering into.

Something tripped him. He groped around on his hands and knees, almost blind, then he blinked the sun-dazzle out of his eyes. He stared at Ma Kruger, who stared back, her eyes wide in terror. Her mouth was open to scream. The wind made a veil that rippled across her face and sand was being driven into her mouth.

It was her body he'd tripped over. She lay on her left side. One hand was still pressed to her right side where her dress was dark with blood.

In a dream once more, Taylor stood and looked around. Mrs Kruger was the first of a trail of dead. They made a pitiful litter at the base of the bluff. The Cameron party. He went numbly from corpse to corpse. He was fearful that the next dead face he looked into would be Fiona Cameron's, but he looked anyway.

A rifle lay at his feet. He lifted it, testing the trigger and found the weapon was jammed.

It was a Winchester 73, the latest model, like the rifle Taylor had owned, although some Apache owned that now. Many rifle shells were scattered around, glittering in the noon sun.

It was clear from how most of the bodies lay that they'd been killed climbing the bluff and had fallen to earth. A long rope hung almost from the top of the bluff, so one of the fleeing people had got that high at least. One man's body hung, upside down, snagged around an outcrop of rock, near to where the tail end of the rope dangled. In his mind's eye Taylor saw the migrants climbing the almost sheer cliff face, whilst Apaches swarmed below, pumping bullets out of their rapid-firing rifles. It must have been a cruel, easy slaughter, people screaming and falling like slaughtered quail.

He found ten dead, six men and four women. Numb and dizzy as he was, it took him a time to work out who wasn't there. All the men were accounted for except Buck Evans and Major Cameron. Four women were missing, including Señora Sanchez. And Fiona Cameron.

There was no sign of any Apache casualties. At any rate, Apaches always carried off their dead.

He did some scavenging, finding a dead man's hat, a bandanna and, most important of all, a canteen that was nearly full. He took a long drink, his first water in twelve hours.

Taylor studied the dim trail zigzagging up the west side of the bluff. He decided he could climb the steep trail unaided three quarters of the way up. After that he'd have to haul himself up the dangling rope, and then it would be a matter of climbing the last twenty yards or so of sheer rock barehanded. He'd have to do that with his head splitting with pain in the eye of the coruscating sun. But he was going to do it anyway, because the six missing people might be lying dead up there, Fiona amongst them.

Some indeterminate time later he was sitting atop the bluff, pouring sweat and feeling the thin air of this altitude sear his chest.

No bodies here, no dead Fiona Cameron. But there were spent cartridges scattered on the earth.

So where were the missing migrants?

The men might have been carried off for torture, the women taken into captivity as spoils of war. It was even possible – although unlikely – that all six missing people had got away.

Off north lay the desert, glaring white in the afternoon haze. Fifty miles in that direction was the Morrison ranch.

Taylor decided he would sleep out the afternoon heat in nearby cover then set out for the Morrison spread at dusk, walking all night if need be.

Far below were the burning wagons and broken bodies of the Cameron party. Taylor stared down at them, the black taste of failure in his mouth. He'd been hired to protect these travellers on their trail of hope. Instead he'd led them to their graves. Already wolves and coyotes were gathering to the feast, and buzzards spiralled down from the sky.

CHAPTER TWELVE

Taylor made his way to a bosky, or grove, of mesquite trees. He found a place to sleep and slept without dreaming.

When he woke it was late afternoon. The aching in his head had eased. He scouted around for food, finding some squaw cabbage to chew, and sucked sweet juice from the pads of a prickly pear. He begrudged the time this took but he had to eat and drink something. Otherwise he wouldn't have the strength to do what he had to do next. He paused from time to time to look for enemies in the surrounding country.

A few columns of pale smoke still climbed out of the box canyon. Taylor watched the smoke and frowned. He filled his pockets with beans from the mesquite trees. As sundown came he moved.

He walked and jogged his way through part of the night. Fortunately there was a sky of stars and he pointed himself at the North one. Around midnight he found some flat ground above a long gravel slope, where he couldn't be sneaked up on easily. There he slept.

He awoke before dawn and watched the sun come up. When that didn't reveal any Apaches, he drank from his canteen, chewing the last of his supply of mesquite beans. Then he started walking once more.

Perhaps, he thought, his luck was turning. About 11 a.m. he found a small water hole, a tank of limpid green water in a cup of rocks, girded by a few cottonwood trees. He drank warm, earthy water, filled his canteen, then climbed into the rocks above the water hole and found shade to sleep in.

This time it was a troubled sleep. He dreamed of Ethan Evans with a fire smouldering on his belly and Fiona Cameron falling screaming from the cliff face.

He woke as the afternoon heat was easing. He went down to the water hole and drank some more. Then he saw dust.

It wisped on the plain to the south, coming towards him, maybe enough dust for half a dozen riders. He waited in cover and watched. There wasn't much else he could do, armed as he was with only a knife. Squinting into the afternoon glare he missed his field glasses, but when the riders got within a rifle shot of him, he had a pretty good idea of who they were.

He stepped from cover, waved his hat and shouted. The newcomers saw him and came towards him.

There were five horsemen, all Anglos. Taylor was surprised to see Jedediah Garth.

Garth was dressed more or less all in black, from his black shirt to his Borsalino hat, which Taylor imagined would be uncomfortable wear in this fierce heat. The others were nondescript men in trail gear, although they were better dressed than the average cowhand. And better armed.

Taylor told them: 'There's been a massacre!'

Garth stared at Taylor grimly. 'We know, son. We come across a survivor...'

'A woman?'

Garth shook his head. 'Fellow named Buck Evans.'

Taylor asked, 'How come you're out here, anyway?'

Garth's party camped by the water hole, with guards out. A fire was lit and a meal cooked. And Garth told his tale.

He'd decided to visit Rio Azul to see what the needs of the new settlement were. He'd organized a mule train of goods, and a crew of a dozen mule-skinners. Travelling partly by night, and by a parallel route to the north of the Trail of Lost Souls, they'd made good time and had no trouble with Indians. Taylor wasn't surprised. Garth's muleskinners looked a tough crew and bristled with weapons.

Garth's company had done good business in Rio Azul, even trading their mules for horses so they could make better time on the return trip. Nothing untoward had happened on the return journey until they'd seen smoke climbing against the sky. Then they'd found Buck Evans staggering around afoot in the desert.

As he listened Taylor sat and ate the food he'd been offered, chewing mechanically, although he had no idea what he was eating. He asked Garth: 'Did he say what happened to Major Cameron, and his daughter?'

Garth shook his head. 'We could get hardly any sense out of him.' He frowned. 'Maybe it's 'cus he was out in the sun too long. Maybe it's what he saw. And then he had to bury his brother ... what was left of him.'

Taylor remembered Ethan the last time he'd seen him and frowned.

Garth scowled. 'Evans took us to where it

happened. We buried those poor people. I wish all those bleeding hearts who feel sorry for the poor noble red man had seen ... what we had to bury.'

Taylor said, 'The dead are dead! There might be five people still alive out here. We should be looking for them!'

Garth studied Taylor with chilly grey eyes. 'Some would say that's a mite callous. As it happens, we are looking. That's how we found you. I sent a rider to the Morrison ranch to get help. Meantime I got another party out looking. Evans is with 'em.'

'Lend me a horse, I'll go join 'em.'

'Mister, these horses need to rest. And so do the men. In a little while we'll get to looking again.'

Taylor wanted to argue but he knew there was sense in what the merchant said. Garth began to roll a cigarette. 'One thing: looked like those Indians in Devil's Pass was damn well-armed. There was Winchester shells all over.'

Taylor started to speak, to tell Garth about the man with jingle-bobs on his spurs. Then it came to him that if he did so, Garth might ask him: *If the Apaches had you prisoner, how'd you manage to escape?* He saw himself telling Garth: *Loco's son set me free because I spared his life.*

Garth lit his cigarette. 'If Loco gets hold of enough repeating rifles, he could take back this whole country.'

'I reckon Loco's band'll run for Mexico. After what they've done here, every blue-coat in the territory'll be after them.'

'Soldiers? You don't see a bluebelly around here from one month to the next.'

'You will now. After this. This country thought the Indian wars were over until Loco reminded 'em!'

Garth gave him a careful, suspicious look. 'You seem to know a lot about Indians. I recall now, you had that Apache belt thing–'

There was a pistol shot. It came from the south. A man standing guard on the south side of the camp said, 'Looks like more of our boys coming in!'

Six horsemen rode up to the camp. Amongst them was Buck Evans.

Evans flinched with shock as he stared at Taylor, as if he saw a ghost. Tonelessly, he said, 'Taylor.'

There was a wild cast to his eyes. Taylor could understand that. Less than a day before, Evans had found what the Apaches had left of his brother, tied to a barrelhead cactus... Taylor could only feel pity for this man.

Evans dismounted. He strode up to Taylor, pausing four or five paces from the other man.

Taylor asked him: 'Where's Cameron, Buck? And his daughter?'

Evans didn't seem to hear the questions. In the same toneless voice as before he said, 'My brother's dead.'

'Your brother was a brave man.'

Evans hands went to his wrists, pulling at fringed gloves that weren't there. Anger came into his face. 'Why ain't *you* dead?'

He needed to blame someone, Taylor knew, as part of the answer to the pain he felt. Evans went on: 'Four of you went up the canyon. The others are dead. Why ain't you?'

Garth dropped his cigarette to the earth and ground it under foot. He gazed at Taylor. 'Just come to me now what that belt is. Some kind of safe passage, ain't it? You show that to Apaches and they let you through.'

Evans took a pace nearer Taylor. 'I heard you talking. Apaches are human beings! That's what you said! Loco got a real bad deal... Apaches have a sense of humour...' Evans's voice caught over the last word. His face became hot and he seemed to be blinking back tears. 'We tossed a coin,' he said to no one in particular. 'We tossed a coin and I won, God help me...'

Most of the faces around Evans were turned towards Taylor, and hostility showed in some of them. A murmuring ran through the onlookers, an ugly sound. Taylor felt a stirring of fear on the back of his arms. He revised his opinion of Garth's muleskinners. He'd thought they were a tough crew. Now he decided they were a *very* tough crew. He wondered where Garth found men like these.

Evans declared: 'Calvin Taylor, the great scout! Calvin Taylor, the Indian-loving son of a bitch!' He seemed to have forgotten about the pistol on his right hip. He balled his hands into fists and took another step forward.

Taylor still felt pity, looking at the anguish in the man's face. 'I don't want to fight you, Buck!'

Garth said, 'There was a Calvin Taylor who was an army scout. Squaw man, they say. Led the army into that Apache ambush at Ghost Mountain over in Arizona. I figured he was an older feller, or somebody had killed him recent... Is that *you*, Taylor?'

It was, but Taylor didn't reply. Garth lifted his voice. 'Speak up, damn you!'

Evans said, 'Ask him why he ain't dead.

How he got out of the canyon.'

Garth did so. 'You fought your way through – that right?'

Taylor nodded. Some of the muleskinners moved forward, crowding towards him. Taylor took two small steps backwards.

Garth posed another question. 'So how come you turn up with no gun? All you had on you was that Apache knife. You get through all them Indians but you lose your guns in the process?'

'That's right.'

'Bullshit.'

One of the muleskinners grinned. 'Maybe we should beat the truth out of him, Jed!'

Garth said, 'I'll tell you what happened, Taylor. They caught you – that's how you got that dandy bruise on your forehead. But they saw that belt and let you go.'

Evans made a strange choked sound of anger and breathed through his nose. Garth went on: 'Let you go and got busy killing the other fellows.'

Which was pretty close to the truth but Taylor said, 'You're goddamned liar!'

Garth said, 'We ain't just got an Indian-lover here, boys. We got us a renegade!'

CHAPTER THIRTEEN

Taylor said, 'You son of a bitch!'

Evans swung.

His right hook caught Taylor high on his left cheek, staggering him. Taylor went to one knee and Evans charged him. He cried out as he charged.

Taylor started to rise and Evans met him halfway, bowling him from his feet, spilling over him in a white fog of dust. They rolled under a horse's belly. The animal shied and whinnied and skittered about. A hoof grazed Taylor's shoulder as the horse danced around him.

Both men writhed in the dust. One of Evans's large, powerful hands grabbed at Taylor's throat, the thumb of his other hand jabbed towards Taylor's eye. Taylor rolled clear. Both men scrambled up. Taylor said, 'I don't want to fight you, Buck!' but Evans charged in again. He swung a wild right that would have broken Taylor's jaw had it connected. He plunged past Taylor, who sprang back, away from his opponent.

Something struck Taylor across the back, above the left hip, knocking him forward. He went to his knees, gasping with pain, one hand going behind him. Over his shoulder he glimpsed Garth grinning, a rifle in his hands. He must have whacked Taylor across the kidneys with the barrel. Other faces showed behind Garth, other muleskinners, and they seemed to be enjoying the show too. Taylor felt a rush of hot anger. He started to rise; then Evans kicked him in the chest.

Taylor seemed to be floating and then turning. And then he was face down in the dust, the taste of blood in his mouth and his chest full of flames. It seemed he couldn't breathe.

He got to his hands and knees. He shook his head, where church bells pealed. He found some air at last and sucked it into his seared lungs.

Evans loomed over him. Triumph showed in his face, his teeth bared in a feral grin. Taylor thought: *maybe I've met my match, maybe I can't beat this man.*

Evans stepped towards him, suddenly breaking into a run. Taylor found the strength to move. He flung himself across the charging man's legs and tripped him. They rolled in dust and came to their feet. Evans swung and missed and Taylor caught him with a right he felt through to his shoulder. He was surprised to see Evans spin and go down. But Evans rose almost immediately, blood on his lips.

Taylor swung a punch, Evans dodged. The swing pulled Taylor forward; as he lunged past Evans the other man looped his arms around Taylor's middle and hugged him close, trapping his arms to his side. Taylor squirmed against the man behind him. Evans linked his hands over Taylor's stomach and began to squeeze. Breath grunted out of him; his arms seemed to surge with a new power.

A band of pain circled Taylor's ribs; he cried out. The bear hug tightened. There was fire in Taylor's chest: he thought he heard one of his ribs begin to crack. He didn't know where Evans found his new strength but titanic force seemed to pour through his arms. *Squeezing like that, Evans would snap his spine.* Taylor felt the sweat of terror on his face and breath began to whine in his throat.

Faces of onlookers spun a dizzy circle around him, like sunspots becoming grinning faces and then sunspots again. He glimpsed

Garth smiling slightly, watching the fight and carefully picking a sliver of meat from between his teeth.

As he squeezed, Evans grunted: 'God damn you, Kolvig!'

Taylor made a last effort; he threw himself backwards, kicking his legs up into the air. It was an attempt to off-balance Evans; it worked. Taylor drove the man holding him backwards. They fell, Evans underneath. Taylor hooked an elbow into the other's throat and heard him gasp. Taylor strained, broke free and writhed to his feet. Evans, one hand to his throat, came upright also. He lunged at his enemy. Taylor seized Evans's head in a necklock, turned and went to one knee, pitching the other man headlong over his shoulder. Evans somersaulted forward, turning once in the air and landed heavily on his back. Air came out of lungs in a long sigh; he lay with limbs outflung.

Taylor swayed. His jaw throbbed and hot flashes of pain ran through his ribs. He was shaking, slick with sweat and dizzy from heat he hadn't noticed.

Evans tried to rise and got as far as lifting his head.

The half-circle of onlookers had stood frozen as the fight resolved itself. Now they moved. Taylor felt a quick stab of fear as muleskinners stepped towards him.

In the same instant Taylor noticed a pistol lying in the dust: Evans's Colt had worked loose from his holster. Taylor snatched it up, cocked and aimed. He put the front sights of the gun on the nearest man.

He said, 'Hold it!'

They halted.

Taylor's mind was racing, trying to think of a way out of this. How could he keep at bay the mob in front of him and still get on a horse and escape? In the same moment of thought it came to him that there were men behind him too...

He heard a sound in the air and turned.

It was a muleskinner, swinging a rifle by the barrel. The blow missed Taylor's face by an inch; the rifle butt caught his right shoulder and drove splitting pain through it. Taylor half-spun backwards, seeing Evans's pistol fall from his nerveless fingers, lost balance and went down on his back. Men were suddenly all around him. He got to his knees and caught a kick in the mouth and went down again. Then he was being dragged upright, his arms pulled behind him and punches rained down on him from all sides. Taylor clung on to dizzy consciousness and then Garth was calling: 'Hold up, boys! Hold up!'

The blows ceased.

The world slowly settled around him. Faces became faces again, not bright revolving orbs. He was aware of where fists and boots had struck him but pain was only beginning there. His main source of hurting was his mouth. A kick had torn his lower lip, which burned fiercely, and had also loosened his teeth. Blood from his split lip had covered the right-hand side of his shirt.

Someone called: 'Let's stomp this fellow!'

Garth said. 'No, boys. This is an Indian-loving renegade.' His voice was calm, reasonable; he might have been discussing the price of flour back in his store. 'And we know how to deal with renegades.'

Men stared. Then they seemed to catch the idea at the same time, and turned their faces to the water hole behind them. Taylor looked too. They looked at the trees there. Most of them were too stunted to serve, but one cottonwood, at the eastern end, was tall and sturdy, with several strong boughs arching out. It might have been designed for a hanging.

CHAPTER FOURTEEN

Taylor thought: *If I'm going to die, I don't want to do it on the end of a rope.*

He'd seen hangings that had been botched, where the victim twisted and strangled slowly. So he strained against the three or four men holding him, even though he knew that doing so was futile. A knee rammed into the middle of his back; air went suddenly out of his lungs and his legs melted below him. Whilst he flopped bonelessly, he was dragged over to the bosky. A muleskinner produced a thick rope and fashioned an expert noose. He slipped the noose over Taylor's head.

The other end of the rope was flung over the cottonwood bough and someone led up a horse. The faces around him looked happy; Jed Garth looked particularly happy. Evans was there.

Garth told him: 'Maybe you want to do the needful, Evans!'

Taylor remembered the last poor devil he'd seen hang: the man's purpling face, his blackened tongue thrusting out between his teeth, his trousers darkening as he voided, a cry juddering out of him like the screeching of an ungreased cartwheel...

Someone called: 'Jed! More riders!'

Garth told the muleskinners: 'Hold it boys.' He moved away from the others and studied the distance to the south through his field glasses. A wind was building, lifting fine dust and dimming visibility, so it was a minute before he lowered the glasses. 'It's old man Morrison.' He seemed to sigh a little. Glancing at Taylor he said, 'Get that noose off him.'

As Taylor was freed of the rope, he swallowed some of the fear in his throat. It was a fair-sized lump; he decided he feared death by hanging more than any other way of dying.

Garth held a Winchester carbine, presumably the same rifle he'd whacked Taylor across the back with. He gestured to a spot nearby with the Winchester's barrel and told Taylor, 'Sit there.'

Taylor obeyed.

Six riders approached. Five men and one woman.

Taylor saw four of the men were dressed like ordinary cowhands, though again, better-armed. Two were Anglos and two Mexicans. The fifth man was Major Cameron, his left arm in a sling. The woman was his daughter, Fiona.

Taylor stood, not realizing he was standing. It was as if some invisible string pulled him to his feet. A dizzy wash of relief went through him.

He was reminded that he was standing when he felt sharp pain behind his left knee and his left leg went from under him. He fell heavily on his left side. Taylor hissed with pain and his hand went to the back of his knee. As he kneaded the sharp aching there, he glared at Garth, who stood over him, smiling. The man shifted the carbine in his hands and said, 'I told you to sit.'

Taylor felt a warm anger that was almost pleasant. There was now a nice tally of indignities to pay this man back for, if he got his chance.

The horsemen reined in at the edge of camp. One man pushed his rosewood bay forward.

Garth walked over to him. He said, 'Eli.'

Eli Morrison was a big name in this quarter of the territory, so Taylor was surprised to see a short man who didn't seem to have much spare flesh on him. Morrison looked nearer sixty than fifty, a grey handlebar moustache dwarfing a narrow face. He had what looked like a cast in his left eye. He wore the dusty trail gear, bandanna, vest and batwing chaps of the cowhands with him; he was in no way better dressed. He swept off his sombrero and showed he was bald, a few wisps of grey hair on his scalp and around his ears. But his eyes were blue and angry, and they fixed on Jed Garth. He said, 'You're still not keeping any better company, Garth.' Taylor decided Morrison's voice had kept its East Texas origins. It also showed his dislike for Garth.

Garth offered a slight, conciliatory smile. 'This is a good outfit, Eli.'

Morrison's lips twisted with contempt. 'What's going on here?'

Garth indicated Taylor. 'We was asking this feller here how come he managed to escape the massacre. We wasn't satisfied with his answer.'

'Is that any reason to hang him?'

'We figure he's a renegade. Did a deal with the Indians to save his own hide.'

Evans put in his two cents' worth. In an angry, choked voice he said, 'Then he left the rest of us to die!'

Cameron said, 'This man was our scout.'

Evans nodded. 'Yeah, and led us into an ambush!'

'Damn you, Evans!' Because of the sling on his left arm Cameron dismounted awkwardly and came forward. The wind pushed against him. His eyes were slitted against it and his bottom lip was thrust forward, his face full of indignation. 'Being ambushed by experts doesn't make you a renegade.'

A muleskinner said, 'Let's hang this Indian-lover!'

Morrison might be small, but Taylor decided he was plenty feisty. The rancher gave the muleskinner a look that would have withered solid rock. 'There'll be no lynching on my land! There's a lot here we need to get to the bottom of, and I intend to get to the bottom of it!'

Garth said, 'I suggest we do it someplace else. Instead of augurin' in the middle of a dust storm.'

Morrison thought a moment, then nodded. 'Your people are welcome to the hospitality of my ranch.'

Garth said, 'I'm obliged, Eli, but the way this wind's building we'll be chin-deep in sand 'fore we get there. The stage station at Agua Dulce's only about eight miles west. A few of my boys might be there.'

Morrison nodded again.

Someone found a horse for Taylor. Garth

observed, 'Best tie him, Eli, in case he bolts.'

Morrison answered with a look of some contempt. 'I don't hogtie folks without reason.' At the same time he showed he had some sense of humour. He told Taylor, 'You can ride up near me, son, keep me company. I wouldn't want you to wander off.'

Camp broke up, people climbed into the saddle. The party moved off. Taylor tried to catch Cameron's eye, or more particularly his daughter's, but both turned their horses and were lost in swirling dust.

A few miles along they came across some more Morrison riders. As these dim figures emerged from wind-blown sand, Taylor saw there was a woman amongst them, barely clinging to her horse.

Lifting his voice over the gale, Morrison asked, 'What you got there, boys?'

One cowhand told him, 'We found her, running round in the desert.' He gazed at Morrison and frowned.

Fiona Cameron said, 'Señora Sanchez!'

Señora Sanchez slipped from horseback and ran forward. But she didn't run to Fiona. Taylor watched in surprise as she ran to him.

Morrison said, 'Get down and greet her, son.'

Bemused, Taylor did so.

She startled him by flinging her arms around him, crying 'Ramon! Ramon!' and bursting into tears.

Morrison said, 'Now don't take on, ma'am. We'll soon get you back to safety.'

Señora Sanchez clung to Taylor, sobbing and crying out in Spanish. He couldn't make out the words at first and then he realized she was crying: 'My boy! My boy! You're safe! You're safe! Thank God! Thank God!'

Taylor took her gently by the shoulders and stepped back, gazing into her face, which appeared and disappeared behind her wind-blown hair. One glance into her eyes told him the likeliest reason she was still alive. Even if the Apaches had captured her, she would have been safe. They feared the insane, and wouldn't harm them.

CHAPTER FIFTEEN

Towards dusk they came into view of Agua Dulce.

Here was an abandoned swing station for a failed stage line. There were a scatter of adobes and a well: one main building and a few smaller outbuildings and huts. In back of that was a corral with high adobe walls on three sides. Here also were three more of Garth's muleskinners.

Two of these men came from the main house and greeted their boss. Riders dismounted and began to enter this building.

Garth pointed with his rifle. He told Taylor, 'After you.'

Taylor set off in the direction Garth indicated and the merchant followed. They passed the corral where a man, the third of Garth's muleskinners, leaned on the mesquite bars of the fence. He was talking to the stock in the corral, making the kind of soothing noises you used to calm snuffy, wind-spooked horses. Garth said, 'Schim.'

Schim turned and said, 'Boss.' He glanced

idly at Taylor and then looked more sharply, as if he recognized him. Taylor couldn't remember seeing this man's long, pale face but Schim seemed to know him, or thought he did. Taylor's heart sank. He thought: maybe here's someone else who knows me from Arizona. Knows me as Calvin Taylor, *the Indian-lover.*

Taylor and Garth moved on and came to a little adobe hut with a flat roof of mesquite thatch.

Once inside the bare, unfurnished hut Taylor was told to sit in one corner. Garth departed. A guard, one of the muleskinners, sat by the steer-hide door and laid his pistol on his lap. He took out his Bible and began to shape a cigarette, reminding Taylor of his craving for tobacco.

There were no windows in this hut to give light so the guard lit a kerosene lamp. Taylor listened to the bleary voice of the wind outside.

Later, Taylor had a visitor: Fiona Cameron.

She brought him a meal, the range staple of bacon, beans and sourdough biscuits, and a cup of coffee. She didn't speak, and barely met his eye, before leaving.

After he ate, Cameron and Morrison came over.

Cameron said, 'Well, Taylor, this is a sorry state of affairs.'

Cameron seemed to have aged ten years on the Trail of Lost Souls. The last days had deepened the lines in his face and whitened his hair. Worse, his eyes, which were once bright with confidence, now seemed either dull or bewildered.

'Nobody's told me, Major, what happened. In Devil's Pass.'

Cameron gazed into space. He rubbed at the sling that held his left arm. 'It was a slaughter. A slaughter.'

He said the last word so low Taylor could barely hear him. He went on: 'We were first, that's why we survived. Myself, Fiona, Buck Evans. We got up to the top of the bluff first. They hit us just as the rest were maybe halfway up. The worst possible time.' Cameron blinked and a tear ran a red trail down his left cheek. 'That'll be with me long as I live. What I heard, what I saw...' There was a little silence. Morrison reached out and rested one hand on Cameron's shoulder. Eventually the Scot found his voice again. 'They just shot us down. They'd got hold of a lot more guns from somewhere. Two days before, you said, they were poorly armed...'

Morrison said, 'Somebody sold 'em guns.'

Taylor's mouth twisted bitterly. 'At least no one's blaming me for that.'

Morrison glared angrily. 'Somebody did, though; sold those Indians guns, may he burn in Hell for it for ever.'

Cameron nodded. 'Wasn't for him, most of us would have climbed that bluff and got away.'

Taylor wondered if he should tell the truth now. But that would still mean revealing why Loco's son had set him free. That would be enough reason for Garth's men, at least, to see him decorating a tree... Anyway, what did he know about the gunrunner? That he wore jingle-bobs on his spurs? So did maybe a quarter of the horsemen in the territory.

Taylor asked, 'How did you get away, Major?'

'I guess most of the Indians were down in the basin. Only a little bunch came after us up on the top. They didn't have Winchesters and we drove 'em off. That's when we got separated from Evans. Wandered round the desert until Morrison here found us. Saved us.'

'You all right ... you and Fiona?'

Cameron touched his sling. 'This'll heal. Fiona didn't get a scratch, thank the Lord.'

The gale outside seemed to ease. A stray draught flickered the flame in the kerosene lamp and shadows stretched on the yellow adobe wall.

Cameron said, 'You were right, Taylor.'

'Major?'

'You said wait until we knew if hostiles were in this country. But I wouldn't wait. I was another Moses, going to lead my people to a promised land. Instead ... I led them all to their deaths.'

'We didn't find one dead child, Major. And some of the women are still missing. Most likely they ain't dead: the Apaches carried them off.'

The steer-hide door creaked as it swung open and Jed Garth entered. He said, 'I don't want to interrupt, gentlemen, but I wondered ... you got anything out of the prisoner?'

Morrison said, 'We were just about to get to that.' He turned to Taylor. 'So what's your story? You just fought your way through?'

'I managed to pull an Indian off his pony. Rode out of the canyon.'

'How'd you lose your rifle and your gun?'

'I dunno. I got a knock on the head somewhere and I can't remember everything.'

Morrison looked at the prisoner in vague

disgust. 'That's kind of thin, son. You're hiding something.'

Taylor's temper flared. 'I don't even know why I'm being held here. What've I done, apart from getting out of Devil's Pass alive?'

'Nothing. Except I've got the feeling if we don't watch you close, you'll take off for parts unknown quicker than a scalded cat.'

Taylor studied the low roof of the adobe rather than meet Morrison's eye. He decided this was a shrewd old bastard, as that was just what he was thinking!

Morrison said, 'Soon as we get back to my ranch, we'll find a county sheriff to hand you over to. He'll decide if you're a wrongdoer or not. You'll get due process of the law.' Morrison addressed Garth. 'That all right by you?'

Hostility was in Morrison's voice but Garth managed a small smile in return. 'Sure, Eli.'

Garth left.

Morrison stared after him in distaste. 'There's another one doesn't seem right. Respectable businessmen ... and yet ... I can tell a rough customer. I wonder what his name was in the States?'

Taylor said, 'I'm obliged, Mr Morrison.'

'What for?'

'If you hadn't showed, Garth's men would have strung me up.'

Morrison glared. 'Don't thank me yet. Maybe I saved an innocent man from getting lynched. Or maybe you are what Garth said – a renegade who led a lot of poor, innocent people to a cruel death. Mr Cameron's people. And justice has just been postponed.' The old man's fierce blue eyes burned into Taylor's and his thin hands clenched into fists. 'Either way, I will, by God, find out.'

As Garth emerged from the hut Fiona Cameron came towards him. He touched his hat and greeted her. She smiled and responded and went on into the hut.

Normally Garth would have let his thoughts dwell on a woman like that. He was a man with an appetite for all the finer things of life. He came from a family that had known wealth, owned land, property and even people before the War destroyed the great house and the plantation, and the carpetbaggers descended like vultures on what was left. He'd been busted down to little more than a field hand and it had been a long fourteen years trying to claw his way back. In the process he became someone who'd forgotten what it was like to wear a new silk shirt each day. Now he wore black sateen, and didn't worry if he hadn't changed his shirt from one day to the next. A man who, to fit in with those around him, said 'ain't' not 'isn't'. One thing that he hadn't lost, however, was his appreciation of fine women.

But he didn't think about Fiona Cameron now. His throat was dry and there was sweat on the palms of his hands. He was afraid, he realized, and had been ever since he'd come across the nightmarish scene in Devil's Pass...

When a figure moved in the gusty darkness before him, Garth's hand went to the cedar grip of the Colt pistol on his hip. Then he saw it was Schim. Garth told himself: *Get a hold of your nerves, damn you, before a bad situation gets even worse!*

Schim said, 'Boss, I need to speak to you. Private.'

Garth nodded.

They found an open-faced shed that might have been used as a smithy. A night guard patrolled nearby, a dim figure behind blown dust, his rifle cradled in his arms, but he was out of earshot.

Schim was a tall man with hair and

moustache so fair it was almost invisible, and pale-blue eyes. They called him Schim because no one could pronounce his long German name. Some of the other men took against him because of the cold deadness of his eyes, which seemed to reflect his cold-heartedness generally. But Garth didn't care about that. He valued Schim more than anyone else in the outfit. There wasn't much Schim was afraid of and not much he wouldn't do, if the money was right. Which was why he was Garth's only partner in the merchant's latest, and most dangerous, venture.

Garth said, 'I think maybe we've got in too deep here, Schim.'

Schim said, 'Boss, that feller you brought in – Taylor.' He lowered his voice so Garth had to strain to hear him from only a few paces away. 'I've seen him before.'

'So?'

Schim was nervous as hell and it showed in his voice. 'I saw him in Loco's camp.'

At the word 'Loco' Garth flinched. He looked for the night guard. The man was still in view, although further away now. Then Garth asked Schim, 'When?'

'When I was delivering the guns.'

Taylor looked up as Fiona Cameron approached. She reached down for the tin plate he'd cleaned, and the tin cup. She showed nothing in her face, and she wouldn't meet his eye.

He saw Cameron and Morrison were in conference by the entrance. Keeping his voice low so they might not hear, he told her, 'What they're saying about me ... it isn't true.'

When she replied it was low too, almost a whisper. 'I know it isn't.'

'Except...'

She was still reaching, but paused. He swallowed, because he didn't want to say what he said next. 'They call me a squaw man. Well, in Arizona, I lived with an Aravaipa Apache girl.'

'White men can't marry Apaches.'

His mouth twisted with irony. 'We wasn't exactly married. So now you know. When they say I'm an Indian-lover, they're right.'

She held still a minute. Then she said, 'I don't care.'

'Sure you don't care?'

She lifted the plate and cup. Somehow, doing that, she managed to brush her left hand across the top of his hands. She glanced at him; he felt a small excitement at the look in her eyes. She said, 'I don't care.'

Schim said, 'They had Taylor tied down and was all set to go to work. So how'd he get free?'

Garth dismissed the question with a small shake of his head. 'Thing is, did he see you?'

'I don't know. I don't think so.'

'But you don't know.'

Garth watched the night guard pacing the low hill above him. His thoughts were whirling, he tried to nail them down and find the one idea in there that might get him out of this mess.

Schim said, 'Maybe we shouldn't've sold that last lot of guns. Loco used 'em a damn sight too well. And a damn sight too soon after he got 'em. Anyone finds out...'

Garth was suddenly confident again. He knew what he was going to do. 'Nobody'll find out, Schim. Taylor hasn't said anything yet.'

'Not *yet* he hasn't. But–'

'And he won't.'

'Boss–'

Garth smiled. 'Down in Mexico – well, you know I hate to say anything good about them damn chilli-eaters, but even a greaser gets a good idea now and then. Like them *rurales,* them Mexican police. What keeps happening to their prisoners. You heard of the law of *ley fuga?*'

Schim got the idea straight away. His face brightened. 'Sure.'

'You're going to draw some guard duty tonight, Schim. Guarding Mr Taylor. Then...'

'Ley fuga.' Schim nodded slightly. 'Killed while trying to escape.'

CHAPTER SIXTEEN

Taylor woke instantly.

He was surprised he'd managed to sleep, on this hard floor, under a few flimsy blankets, in the chill of the night, with the banshee keening of the wind outside. But he had because the darkness around him was thicker and blacker, and the wind had fallen to a sullen moan.

So what had awakened him?

It had been the creak of the steer-hide door opening.

And something else, another sound.

The air was still cold and he moved his numbed hands to get life back into them. He gazed towards the doorway and a piece of the darkness moved, formed shape and became the silhouette of a man standing over him, face and features in shadow. Taylor determined that the bar across the man's body was a rifle.

This man whispered, 'Come on.'

Taylor sat up. He'd slept in his clothes, apart from his moccasins, which he pulled on now.

His faceless companion made an impatient sound and gestured with the rifle towards the door. Taylor couldn't identify him from his outline or his voice, yet something about him was familiar. Taylor felt uneasy, and maybe afraid. Was this man taking him to safety? Or to vigilante justice outside the adobe, a bullet or a hanging tree?

Taylor whispered: 'What is–'

'Shut up and move!'

The man's voice showed his nerves were stretched tight as rawhide. So that made two of them.

Taylor stood. He crossed the room to the door and paused there. The barrel of the rifle poked hard into his back, just above the waist, and he stumbled forward, out into the night.

There was a strong full moon, white as bone, silver-plating the ground before him. The land was a chequerboard of black and silver, blurring at the edges as a low, persistent wind raked brush and trembled shadows. Both he and the man behind him, framed in the doorway, held still, listening.

It was very silent. Then a horse coughed and sneezed in the corral. Taylor heard a few small sounds that didn't fit with the night, off to the left. He found he was studying a low hill where clumps of ocotillo and mesquite swayed with the wind.

The man behind him said: 'Come on. We got a horse waiting.'

Taylor didn't believe him. His ears told him that something – maybe a man – was hidden in the brush atop the low hill. He recoiled from the black and silver ground before him. He saw himself being shot down as he crossed it. It gaped like the mouth of a trap. A gnawing in his guts told him death waited there. *His death.*

The rifleman stepped forward. His boots made a soft rushing sound coming down on gravel, and then there was the sound Taylor had heard as he woke: the clear, ringing music of a jingle-bob spur.

Taylor flung himself backwards.

He crashed into the man behind him, slamming him back against the wall, the rifle trapped between them. Taylor swung full about, linking both hands, bringing them against the side of the other's head. The man reeled and almost fell. Taylor grabbed the rifle; they strained for possession of the weapon, swaying together. Taylor fell backwards, yanking the other towards him. He hit on his shoulders, hooking his feet into the man's belly then straightening his legs. The man flipped into the air, turned headlong and came down on his back. Air grunted out of him.

The rifle spun across loose stones, skittering into shadows.

Taylor squirmed from the earth. His opponent was tough all right; despite his hard fall he was first to his feet. He was a silhouette rising against the stark moon. His right arm was upraised and there was a knife in his hand!

Taylor came to a crouch; he dodged as his enemy stabbed down. The man lunged past him and ploughed to one knee. Taylor lifted his right knee, catching the other alongside the head and knocking him back on his rump. Taylor stood. His opponent started to rise and Taylor kicked out. His foot caught the other's jaw with a meaty, satisfying smack. The man toppled and lay on his back, groaning softly.

Taylor held still a moment, breathing hard. He glimpsed the rifle, lying half a dozen paces away, and stepped towards it.

Something struck him across the back of the right shoulder, driving him forward. He spun and hit on the same shoulder and cried out in pain. He rolled to his feet.

He heard the sound of the shot fading. His attention was pulled to the hill where the wind shook arms of ocotillo and mesquite, to a drift of powder smoke there.

There was a numbness in his right shoulder and damp on his back that might be blood. But fear and excitement pumped through him. He began to run towards cover. He ran Apache style, zigzagging, crouched low. There was another shot but he wasn't hit.

Garth fired twice.

His first shot knocked Taylor down. But Taylor rolled off the earth and started to run, dodging as he did so. Garth drove another shot at the weaving runner. And missed. Taylor made it into cover, vanishing there.

Garth swore. He saw his plan falling to pieces in front of him. His arms trembled with the anger he felt at Schim, at Taylor, and at himself.

But his calm reasserted itself. It always did. Nothing licked him, because he'd always keep his nerve, always think his way through whatever difficulty arose.

As he walked down slope a new plan was already forming in his mind.

Schim climbed groggily to his feet, both

hands to his jaw. Garth heard voices, lights showed in the windows of the main adobe as the shots brought the camp awake. In a few minutes they'd be down here; he had that much time to start his new plan rolling...

Schim turned his dazed face towards Garth. Blood was coming out of his mouth, leaking down his chin. In a voice that seemed half full of water he asked, 'You get Taylor?'

'No.'

Garth saw a knife lying on the earth. Schim saw it too, bent and picked it up. Stooped forward, he must have heard something and glanced back over his shoulder. Surprise showed for an instant in the pale eyes. Then the rifle butt caught his right temple at the end of its swing. Schim fell and lay limply on his face.

Garth knelt over the unconscious man. He took the knife and raised it. For one second he paused, hearing his breathing, hearing the blood beating in his head. He spent that long thinking what he was going to do; then he drove the knife in to the guard. He'd killed like this before. He knew which ribs to place the blade between, and how to twist the knife as it went home.

There were lots of advantages to knifing an unconscious man, Garth decided. For example, if you were careful, you didn't get any blood on you. And Garth was careful.

He left the knife embedded, thrusting up from the dead man's back. He considered that a nice touch.

Taylor ran for some minutes. Then he paused in cover, and listened.

Sounds travelled far in this clear night. He could hear voices back at Agua Dulce.

He put his hand to the back of his right shoulder and flinched with pain. His fingers came away bloody, and his back was damp with it. But he judged this was another crease, barely breaking the skin. He kept running into back-shooters whose aim was slightly off.

He heard hoofs knock against stone.

Taylor moved up a ramp of ground, into a circle of small boulders atop this ramp. He focused his eyes on the ground ahead, trying to see through a screen of mesquite and other brush. False dawn was paling the eastern skyline. A large, irregular shape swam up against this hazy darkness. It became a man on a horse, a night guard drifting his horse towards him and Agua Dulce and the gunshots and noise there.

Taylor crouched, his muscles tensed. That brought sharp pain to his shoulder, which he ignored. He watched the rider loom nearer until he was passing below the very place where Taylor lay. Taylor remembered a trick Nachay had shown him and flung a rock, which clattered on stones to the east. The rider turned suddenly, looking that way, and Taylor sprang. He had better luck than Nachay, he carried the man easily from the saddle and left him sprawling, winded, on the trail. Taylor took the man's pistol from his holster. As the dismounted man lifted his head, Taylor laid the pistol barrel across it. The man sighed and lay stunned. Taylor took his hat, knife, gun and gun belt. He'd drawn a full house: early light showed a Winchester in the saddle boot and a canteen hanging from the saddle horn. Taylor mounted the man's bay horse and rode.

Dawn showed them the full, grim picture. A man lying with a knife thrusting from low in his back.

Four of them stood over the corpse and stared down: Garth, Morrison, Cameron, Buck Evans.

Morrison asked Garth, 'You found him?'

Garth nodded gravely. 'I was coming over to check on poor old Schim here and I saw some feller running for it. I seen his face in the moonlight. It was Taylor. I took a couple of shots at him but he got away.'

He thought his story sounded a little thin but Morrison didn't question it. His eyes were on the dead man at his feet. He chewed at his lower lip and a pulse of fury throbbed in the side of his scrawny neck.

Evans knelt for a moment, feeling the earth, then stood. There was blood on his fingers. 'You winged him, anyway.'

Morrison turned his attention to Cameron. 'Well, you still want to speak up for this feller?'

Cameron gave him a helpless, stricken look.

Morrison said, 'We won't even wait to see the burying. We'll get after him right away. Maybe he won't get far, wounded as he is. One of my hands, Benito, he's part Navajo. He can trail a man over bare rock.'

Garth asked, 'Due process of the law, Eli?'

Morrison fixed the other man with his fierce blue eyes. 'I stopped one man from being hung. Because of that, another lies dead here.' He moved his gaze to the corpse at his feet. 'A mistake I won't make again.'

CHAPTER SEVENTEEN

Taylor came to water.

There was a tank at the base of a sheer rock wall, where there was also a little miraculous green, a fringe of verdure from which birds started. It was the only touch of colour in a narrow, sun-blasted canyon. Taylor was uneasy in this place, because it would be too easy to be trapped in here, but he and his horse needed water. There was only a mouthful left in the canteen he'd stolen.

The tank held run-off water, tasting of the bare rock it had trickled down. In the pool it was green and earthy. But it was easy to dream it was the coldest water ever, pearly liquid from a clear mountain stream, icy on his bloated tongue, whose running music played in his head while he drank.

He ached into his bones, especially his rump and thighs. He'd been almost all day in the saddle. For maybe ten miles, as he fled the ambush outside the hut, he'd run his horse hard, to get some distance on the pursuit he knew would develop. Then he set

154

about laying a false trail, judging that that was time well spent. But it wasn't. Ten miles further on, as he'd glanced back, he'd seen trails of dust following. He hadn't lost his pursuers. One of them, at least, was a damn good tracker.

Taylor had driven the bay horse hard, across the flats and into the first slopes of the mountains. But the animal had been tired to begin with, and its pace was slow. The bay was staggering when they came to water, making the wheezing noises that suggested it was ruined. By which time it was close to darkness, and both man and horse needed to rest.

Taylor ate the last of the jerky he'd found in the saddle-bags, and also some mesquite beans and squaw cabbage. There were signs of jackrabbits by the water hole, also wild pigs and mule deer, but he hadn't time to hunt. He didn't dare make a fire, with pursuers maybe close behind. He felt a little weak and light-headed from hunger, but these last few days he'd got used to travelling on an almost empty belly.

As he chewed his cold rations mechanically he tried not to think of his hunger. He thought about his plan, such as it was: to turn himself in to a county sheriff.

He'd found himself fleeing south. The nearest county sheriff in that direction was in Ore City. Taylor didn't fancy his chances there – what kind of justice would he get in a rough mining camp, where Jed Garth was a big operator? The likelihood was he'd be turned over to a lynch mob. So, with pursuit barring him from the north, he'd have to keep going south and south-west until Mesilla. That was maybe a hundred miles across bad country, mountain and desert, so whether he could make it was anybody's guess.

He realized pursuit had driven him back on his own journey, almost on to the Trail of Lost Souls. He was now pushing into the eastern edges of the Superstitions. He might only be ten miles from Devil's Pass.

Taylor lay under his blankets. He'd sleep until dawn, then strike out for Mesilla and, with luck, a way out of this crazy business.

He dreamed bad dreams. He watched a grim parade of ghosts pass by: the four Williams brothers, Harrison father and son, Ma Kruger, Frau Veidt, Ethan Evans and others, all the people he'd led to their deaths in Devil's Pass ... last of them all Ramon Sanchez... And Ramon Sanchez was staring at him now, as Taylor came awake.

But he couldn't be. Ramon had been dragged to his death behind a running pony. But there he was, copper-skinned and his jet hair cut short, dressed in the white cotton pants and serape of a Mexican peasant.

Then Taylor saw Ramon's face was aged, weather-seared and deeply lined and the long moustache that drooped over his mouth was grey at its tips. This wasn't Ramon but another man, dressed Mexican, another man of Mexican and Indian blood, but old enough to be Ramon's father. Behind him pink light painted the canyon walls, which told Taylor he'd overslept: it was dawn. He lifted his head and the other man moved too, lifting a Winchester carbine and training the black eye of the carbine on Taylor's face.

Other figures loomed behind this man. As each appeared, Taylor felt a new load of fear and despair settle like a cold stone in his belly. Eli Morrison, Buck Evans and Jedediah Garth.

They were all armed but only Garth had a pistol in his hand, not particularly pointed at Taylor. He said, 'Put both hands behind your head. Slow. Get to your feet and kick away those blankets.'

Taylor obeyed.

Morrison asked Taylor, 'You figured you'd got away, huh?' He indicated the Mexican. 'This is Benito. Just about the best tracker in the territory.'

Garth said, 'Search him, Buck.'

Evans did so. He glared at Taylor with hatred. As he finished searching, his mouth twisted and he swung. His right fist caught Taylor on the chin and knocked him flat.

Taylor lay dazed for a moment, then he lifted his head and stared up at Evans. Taylor guessed the man was repaying him for, amongst other things, the fight at the water hole. So he was puzzled when Evans said, 'You murdering bastard!'

'I never murdered nobody.'

'Tell that to Schim!' Seeing the blank look Taylor gave him, he said, 'That feller you knifed in the back, outside the adobe!'

'I didn't knife anyone in the back!'

'You're a goddamned liar!' Evans lifted his fist again.

Morrison said, 'All right! That's enough of that!'

Taylor got to his feet. He nursed his jaw. He decided that Evans had a considerable punch on him. He spat and there was blood in his spittle. 'That feller was alive when I left him.'

Garth scowled. 'We aren't gonna stand here listening to any more of your lies! Due process of the law, Eli?'

'He'll hang all right.'

Garth turned the Colt in his hand. 'Why bother with a hanging?'

Morrison gazed at the other man coldly. 'No, we'll do it halfway legal, at least.'

The merchant sighed. 'Then we need to find us a tree.'

Taylor was led at gunpoint a few hundred yards up the canyon, to where horses were picketed. Garth produced some cotton rope and tied Taylor's hands before him. He tied them tighter than he needed to, smiling slightly when he did so. Taylor filed this away in his mind as another little score to settle with Garth in the future. Of course, that depended on Taylor having a future...

They mounted, Taylor back into the saddle of the bay. The riders moved off, walking their horses west along the canyon.

Benito rode well ahead of the others, on point. They came out of the canyon into a basin. This wasn't a box, like the place where the Cameron party had been trapped and had died. On the far, west side of the basin, there was a way out, a narrow slit in the rock wall where the canyon continued.

Evans brought up the rear. Taylor rode ahead of him, just behind Morrison and Garth. Garth turned in the saddle and asked Morrison, 'How come there ain't never a tree when you want one?'

Taylor studied the basin walls. There was some timber higher up, but they would have to climb steep slopes to come to it. Maybe they'd find a sturdy enough juniper or white oak further along apiece ... that was all his future amounted to: the amount of time it took to find a tree you could hang a man from.

A canyon wren was finishing off its morning song. It looked forward to a better morning than he did. He realized he'd been scanning his surroundings without seeing them. This basin had different strata of rock banding its orange cliffs, tidelines of yellow, green, blue, purple and a mix of these colours. It was a picture of harsh, primitive and startling beauty. He supposed the wren's song was beautiful too, part of the world he was about to be separated from.

He thought: *If I'm going to die, I don't want to do it on the end of a rope.* He didn't want to die at all. He decided there was too much he didn't want to let go of just yet. He remembered Fiona Cameron, the last time he'd seen her. What was in the look she gave him? The promise of something? Maybe the promise of a hell of a lot...

Morrison told Garth, 'Perhaps we should join up with Cameron's bunch, before we do this.'

Taylor asked, 'Major Cameron's out here?'

Morrison looked at him sourly. 'Wasn't talking to you.' Anger made a quiver in the side of the rancher's neck. 'You've caused plenty trouble to everybody. We got all of Garth's outfit and most of my hands out looking for you. Major Cameron's with 'em. They're back in these hills someplace.'

Garth made an exasperated sound. 'Eli, you know that Cameron. He's soft on this feller. We join up with him, he'll be arguing for a sheriff, not a hanging!'

Morrison nodded. 'And it could be he's right. Could be I'm in the wrong here.' Then Morrison seemed to lose interest in this argument, his attention shifted forward and he frowned.

Taylor followed his gaze. In the mouth of the canyon, off to the west, dust showed. Hoofs drummed. A rider issued from the canyon.

It was Benito and he was running his horse towards them at full gallop.

The Mexican was yelling something. But Taylor didn't need to hear the words.

He saw them.

Dust vomited into the basin like surf on to a beach. Seeds of darkness in this dust became men on horseback. He heard distant yelling, and the crack of rifles.

No one yelled orders or instructions. The Morrison party seemed to react automatically: they wheeled their mounts. They struck at their horses with spur and quirt and broke for the east as one man. Taylor spun the bay and was almost bowled over as Buck Evans flashed past him. Taylor spurred his horse and followed Evans's dust.

The bay found its stride and Taylor began to close the distance to the men galloping ahead. Then they reined in, turning their horses in a smother of dust.

Taylor could see why. What he'd seen in the canyon mouth to the west he now saw mirrored in the canyon entrance to the east: dust spewing into the basin, riders in the dust, men with rifles in their hands, coming at him, yelling their fierce cries.

It wasn't real, he decided. This was a dream, a recurring one, the same thing happening again: he was in a high-walled basin, trapped by Apaches.

CHAPTER EIGHTEEN

The horsemen milled in dust. Taylor glanced around, looking for a place to fort up. But Morrison seemed to make the decision for them. He spurred to the north and Garth and Evans followed; then Taylor followed *them*.

He found he was driving the bay upslope, whilst he tried to close his ears to the yelling and rifle fire behind him. The slope became steep and the bay began to rear and paw as ground turned loose under foot. He saw the others above him, piling from their horses. They made no attempt to hold their animals, but let them flee, except Evans who was attempting to get his rifle out of his saddle boot. He had a time of it as his horse danced about. Taylor used his knees to urge the bay to climb higher. Suddenly it reared, neighing crazily, and went over. Taylor hit the hard ground on his side and rolled as the horse toppled towards him. He missed being pinned under its crushing weight by inches; the bay scrambled to its feet and bolted.

Taylor rose, coughing in dust. He glimpsed Benito galloping across the flats below with Apaches on his heels. The Mexican struck the first rising ground. Rifles crackled. His horse reared, screaming, and fell, spilling the rider. Benito staggered to his feet and started to run upslope.

Taylor ran upslope too. There was rifle fire from above and below. Bullets keened. He raced through this crossfire, dodging between rocks and brush. Thorns raked him. His feet churned shale, he lost footing and sprawled on a steep slope that suddenly became loose stones. He slithered downhill in an avalanche of this stuff. He slid some yards, then began to climb again. There was stinging pain on his chin where he'd scraped off skin, the taste of blood and dust in his mouth. He came to rocks and the slope became easier. He climbed until he had to pause to breathe, his heart big as a cannonball and trying to hammer its way out of his chest. He glanced back.

Benito was a hundred yards below, in tangled brush. Above Benito was a bare slope and then the rocks where Taylor crouched. Benito ducked down, almost hugging the earth, because Apache bullets lifted dust all around. Then he broke from cover, running upslope. He ran zigzagging, Apache style, as bullets whined about him. He was halfway to cover, three quarters. Then he was spilling forward, hitting on his shoulder and rolling on. He fetched up almost at the first of the rocks.

Taylor sprang downslope. Benito was down on all fours at his feet. Taylor heard bullets chew into the rocks around him, singing viciously past his head. He bent and grabbed the Mexican's arm, lifting the limb awkwardly because his hands were tied together. Benito leaned against Taylor, his legs failing. Taylor ducked under Benito and the man sprawled across his shoulders. Taylor stood, Benito draped over his back like a sack of feed. Taylor carried the man upslope. He stumbled and went to his knees once or twice. Something yowled in Taylor's ear and stung his cheek, fetching blood, but he kept climbing.

Then Morrison was on the slope above him, standing with legs braced, his rifle pulled into his shoulder as he fired. Taylor and his burden staggered past the rancher and entered a roughly square piece of ground bounded by small boulders. Here the others huddled, firing their rifles downslope. Taylor eased Benito down gently on his side. Then Taylor sat, putting his back against a boulder.

Morrison appeared and sank into cover too. For a minute both Apaches and Anglos were firing as fast as they could pump their rifles.

And then there was silence.

In Taylor's ears it was a pretty noisy silence, a tin plate clattering as it fell on a table, the sound ringing on and on. His arms trembled. Things had happened too fast for him to be conscious of fear before but he was aware of it now. It was back in its usual place, a lump of granite blocking his throat, a high singing in his ears, a cold rottenness in his belly.

He gazed around him. The five men were on a shoulder of level ground jutting out of the slope, skirted with boulders and brush. The tallest rocks and boulders he immediately named the 'Front Rocks', a sort of stone palisade. They made the front ramparts of their little fort, looming over the slope below and to the west. To the east the shoulder backed against an almost sheer granite wall. He crossed their little square of open ground – he christened that the 'Compound' – to the Front Rocks. He gazed down through a narrow slit between two tall boulders. He saw Apaches moving, afoot and on horseback, at the base trot of the slope, out of range. A few of them called out derisively.

Evans asked Morrison, 'You hit?'

Morrison touched his right arm, which was bloody. He hissed and sucked in his teeth but said, 'Just a nick.' The others checked themselves for wounds. Garth and Evans were uninjured. Taylor found there was blood on his chin from the scrape, and more on his face where a bullet had nicked his cheek, but was otherwise unhurt. For all that there seemed to be at lot of blood on the right side of his shirt, soaking it through.

Evans called, 'Hey, Morrison. Your greaser friend!'

Morrison crouched over the Mexican. He said, 'Benito.'

He lifted his face, grey with pain and shock, to Taylor.

Taylor saw Benito was dead. A bullet had caught him in the back of the head and exited through the right cheek. Maybe the same bullet that had raked Taylor's own right cheek, as he'd carried his burden upslope. In which case that might be bits of brain glued to the blood on his shirt. Thinking of that, and looking at the bloody ruin of the dead man's face, Taylor felt his stomach tighten.

Garth said, 'Well, Taylor, looks like you was a big hero for nothing! You drug a corpse in here!'

Morrison pulled off his canvas jacket and laid it over Benito's head and torso. He told Taylor, 'This was a good man and you tried to save him. I'm beholden.'

'Then cut me loose! If I'm going to die, do I have to do it with my hands tied? Give me a rifle and let me fight!'

Garth smiled. 'No chance. You'd turn your gun on us, then go join your Indian friends!'

Morrison looked doubtful, as if he was thinking about it; then he returned to his place at the Front Rocks.

Garth stared up at the wall above and behind them. He said, 'They get above us, they can drop rocks down on us, and sniper down.'

Morrison observed, 'It'll take 'em a time getting up there. Meantime, Cameron and the others are somewhere near. They'll have heard the firing. If they come quick enough, we might get out of this all right.'

Taylor moved to what he already considered his place at the Front Rocks and gazed down. The slopes immediately below were fairly steep and bare of cover, with a good field of fire. He told Morrison, 'You picked a good place here.'

Garth sneered. His lips twisted and he spat, accurately, at a rock. 'Sure, everything's just dandy.'

Garth watched Apaches moving at the bottom of the slope. He shaped what might be his last cigarette. He noted that his fingers trembled slightly, but that was all right. He was still keeping his nerve. Nothing licked him. That was what Garth always told himself. But just maybe this time Loco *had* licked him.

There had been a moment, when the Apaches jumped them, when he had a choice. He might have taken off for open country by himself and left the others to it. If Apaches cornered him he might have had time to tell them: *You don't want to kill me, I'm the man sells you guns!*

But it was hard reasoning with a fellow in the middle of a fight, when bullets flew and blood ran hot. Most likely the Apaches would have cut him down before he had a chance to speak. Or they might be broncos in Loco's band who didn't know him. They might not even be part of Loco's band, but another bunch of renegades, maybe out of Mexico.

So he'd chosen to stay with Morrison. And run the risk of getting killed by his own clients. If these Apaches recognized him now, fighting against them, they'd be less than happy about another treacherous white eye; he'd better not let them take him alive!

Still, he could smile at the irony of being shot by his own guns...

Evans lifted his canteen. He'd found time to bring this with him. He drank. 'They're moving into cover down there. How many of 'em, you figure?'

Morrison had also salvaged his canteen; he drank.

'Seen twenty or so.'

The heat trapped between these rocks was already fierce and would soon be sickening. Garth felt sweat squeezing out of every pore under his dark clothes. The defenders only had two canteens between them and they'd dry out in a few hours. The dead Mexican's body would bloat and become flyblown, the stench unbearable. This place would be a torture box, come noon. But Garth wasn't worried about any of that. The Apaches should have settled them before the sun got halfway to noon. He wondered what was holding them up. He lifted his head, peeking over the rocks and an Apache took a shot at him. The sniper didn't come close but Garth ducked anyway.

He asked nobody in particular: 'You figure this is Loco's band? You see him out there?'

Taylor said, 'No. But it's his band all right. I spotted one of 'em I know from the Mescalero agency. Feller named Kesus.'

'I thought you said the Apaches had run off to Mexico, Mister Indian expert!'

'They make a habit of not doing what they're supposed to.'

Evans rubbed his chin. 'What do you figure they will do? Are they gonna rush us, Taylor? They got the stomach to come at us across that slope? I thought you said they hadn't the guts for that kind of fighting.'

'It wasn't me said Apaches ain't got guts! They'll come. You'll see.'

Evans fixed him with a look of hatred. 'You ain't changed, have you? Even now you're still an Indian-lover!'

Garth exhaled smoke and watched it drift towards the far side of the basin. He flipped the husk of his cigarette after it. 'He's right, though. They'll come, once they've made

their medicine and such.'
   'You reckon?'
   'We'll have 'em in our laps in a minute!'

CHAPTER NINETEEN

But a minute passed and no attack came. Evans stood and peered over the boulder in front of him. 'What are they waiting for?'

Garth was gazing downslope too. 'They're bunching down there, getting ready. Cameron better get here quick, he wants to find us alive.' He spat and grinned. 'Come on, you red bastards!'

Taylor felt a quick stab of admiration for Garth, his arrogance in the face of death. He might be a son of a bitch, like Evans, but there was no doubting either man's courage. Taylor said, 'They're just waiting until they're in place, above us.'

Evans sneered. 'Suddenly you know what they'll do, after all.'

'I can make a fair guess. They'll start sneaking up on us. Draw our fire to get us to waste our bullets. Once they're in position, they'll hit us all at once, from above and below. Swarm all over us. And when that happens, three guns won't be enough. So give me a rifle!'

Evans declared, 'We ain't arming no mur-
derer!'

'I didn't murder that Schim feller.'

'Then who did?'

That was a good question, Taylor decided.
If he had the time he'd ponder it. But time
was something he'd run out of. There might
only be twenty Apaches out there, but that
would be enough. Normally they wouldn't
risk the casualties they'd likely take in a
frontal assault on this place, but maybe this
little party of white eyes was just too temp-
ting a target.

Even if he got out of this bind, Taylor
remembered there was still a rope waiting
for him. It took a man with a remarkable
talent for making enemies to find himself
under siege, and in mortal danger, from
both attackers *and* defenders. It was a
shame every deck was stacked against him,
and death was waiting whichever way he
turned, because he'd just lately come up
with some good reasons to stay alive.

One good reason in particular.

The crack of a rifle brought him from his
thoughts.

Garth said, 'Here they come!'

Firing started. Taylor shifted his position
in the Front Rocks, peering through the

narrow slit between boulders at the slope below. He saw dark cottony bursts of powder smoke and heard lead strike these rocks and snarl about them. He glimpsed Apaches dodging between cover, moving upslope, lifting to fire, then vanishing. They were yelling, to hold up their own courage and put fear into their enemies. They made the yipping, ki-yi-ing sounds of squabbling coyotes. One or two shouted obscenities, in Spanish or English, as there was no profanity in the Apache tongue.

The defenders fired as though they had all the ammunition on Earth. The air grew thick with powder smoke and its too-sweet smell. Evans reloaded. 'You can't hit the bastards, they're too fly!'

Taylor called, 'I told you! They're just getting you to waste your bullets! Try to get ricochets in 'em!'

Morrison came alongside him. He put his back to a boulder and started thumbing shells into the face plate of his Winchester. Taylor lifted his tethered hands. 'Cut me loose, Morrison!'

Garth cried, 'No you don't, Eli!'

As he spoke, bullets chewed into the rocks around him. Garth gasped and one hand went to his ear, as though he was slapping a biting insect; then he slewed around and returned fire.

Taylor said, 'Morrison!'

The rancher gave him his fierce blue eyes. He stared a moment. Then he produced a knife and cut through Taylor's bonds.

Taylor found the spare Winchester in the outfit. He took Benito's cartridge belt. As firing intensified Taylor kneaded life back into his wrists and hands. Then he fed shells into the Winchester and moved alongside Morrison, looking for targets below.

There was firing from a scatter of boulders at the bottom of the bare slope. Taylor studied that for a moment, as best as he could; then he started firing, trying to angle ricochets in amongst the rocks. He tallied: an Apache yelled and jerked up out of cover, his hands to his back. Evans shot him through the face.

Taylor put his back to a boulder, re-loading. As he thumbed the last shell home, dust spumed from the rock besides him and there was a noise like an angry wasp in his ear. Instinctively Taylor glanced upwards. At the top of the rock wall behind and above him, maybe a hundred yards up, was a dark drift of powder smoke! And then another!

Taylor called, 'Morrison!'

Taylor ran across the Compound and flattened against a tall boulder on the east side. Morrison was suddenly at his side. Both men fired upwards. Taylor saw more powder smoke high on the rock wall and drove shots towards it. A bullet plucked at his hat brim. One man came loose from the top of the rock wall and plummeted towards them. Another spilled over the edge and seemed to hang there, head down, poised to dive. Taylor fixed him in his sights and squeezed the trigger. The hammer punched an empty chamber. Taylor grabbed for more shells in his cartridge belt. Morrison kept firing. The Apache hung there a moment more; then he fell.

Taylor heard yelling and firing close behind him. He turned. He saw Evans and Garth firing downslope and then Apaches were coming over the Front Rocks. Taylor glimpsed his old friend Kesus. Kesus sprang at Garth and tackled him to the ground. Another man ran at Evans. Evans grabbed his rifle by the barrel, swung and missed; the Apache ducked and Evans pitched over him. Evans rolled on the earth and the Apache plunged down on him, a knife flashing in his hand.

Another Apache sprang into the Compound, pulling his rifle to his shoulder as he charged forward. Morrison shot him and the man went to his knees. But as he fell he fired. Morrison grunted, spun half-about, then went down.

Taylor took his empty rifle by the barrel and ran towards the fray. He yelled. Evans and the Apache both reared to their knees and strained together, fighting over the one knife. The Apache won. He drove the knife down into Evans's chest. Evans gasped and fell. By which time Taylor was on them. He stood over the combatants, beginning to swing the rifle in its deadly arc to the Apache's skull. He heard a small sound behind him and half-turned. There was sharp pain near Taylor's temple and then he was down on his back.

He didn't quite lose consciousness but lay stunned. He blinked, staring up stupidly. After some time he determined that there was an Apache standing over him, legs straddled, a stone-headed club upraised in his hand.

Taylor tried to move but could find no strength. All he could do was lie and watch.

He saw some strange things.

He saw another Indian rise to his feet, Evans's assailant. There was blood all over this man's long shirt but maybe it was Evans's blood. Both Apaches gazed down at Taylor. He waited for one of these men to kill him. To begin looting the camp, at least.

Instead they turned and ran.

He became aware that all the Apaches had gone. Except Kesus. He remained, locked in combat with Garth.

Taylor watched the fight, curiously dis-interested.

Garth was flat on his back and Kesus knelt on top of him, pinning Garth's shoulders and arms under his knees. Kesus lifted his knife.

Another strange thing happened. Kesus seemed to freeze, with his knife upraised. As he stared down at his victim, there was surprise in his face.

There was a shot: Kesus was torn around and flung backwards.

Taylor glimpsed Morrison sitting up against a rock, shirt bloody and his pistol raised.

Sometime later, in a period of strange quiet, Taylor got to his feet. Bodies lay around him: Evans, Garth, Morrison, Benito, Kesus. Were they all dead? He seemed to be the only thing moving. Dazed, he made his way to the Front Rocks. A dead Apache lay on the slope below the rocks.

He saw living Apaches too. Two men looked to be badly wounded; they were being half-carried and half-dragged down slope by more limber companions. At the base of the slope other Apaches, maybe eight or so, were climbing on to their ponies. They moved off to the west at the half-gallop, towards the canyon mouth.

He wondered why.

Perhaps an answer came just then. A mirror flashed silver high on the varicoloured wall of the basin. Another mirror signalled a reply from near the west canyon.

Taylor returned to the Compound. Some of the dead had miraculously returned to life. Evans and Morrison were both sitting up against rocks. Garth stood, tying his bandanna as a bandage across his temples. Blood from a scalp wound was running down the right side of his face and on to his black shirt. Taylor told him, 'They're pulling out.'

'Why? Is it Cameron's party coming?'

Taylor shrugged. He ought to feel relief, he supposed, but he was too dazed, maybe from the blow on the head, to feel much of anything.

Garth declared, 'It sure wasn't us scared

'em off. They had us cold.'

Taylor regained some sense; he managed to do a tally of the damage. He and Garth had got off lightest: Taylor had been knocked silly by a war club, whilst Garth had a bullet graze in his forehead and a bloody notch in his ear. Morrison had been shot in the side. He was in considerable pain but still lucid and reckoned he'd been shot through, the bullet wasn't in him. It was hard to gauge how badly he was hurt but the wound didn't look fatal.

Evans appeared to be dying.

The knife wound in the left side of his chest had left him soaked through in blood. His face was grey. He seemed to be trying to speak but couldn't, only blood came from his mouth. His eyes said he knew. Taylor gazed at him and was surprised at the sorrow he felt. Evans had a pistol in his hand, the weapon resting on his thigh as if he hadn't the strength to lift it. He gripped it so tightly his knuckles shone white, as if he expected the Apaches to return any minute.

When Taylor heard a voice behind him he nearly jumped out of his skin.

Kesus said almost the only English words he knew.

'Shadow Man.'

CHAPTER TWENTY

Kesus was trying to raise his head.

Garth lifted his rifle and trained it on the wounded man.

Taylor said, 'Hold it!' He stepped between Garth and the Indian.

Garth made a sound of disgust. 'You're still the same – still an Indian-lover!'

Taylor ignored him and crouched over Kesus.

The Apache was a stocky young man whose face was badly pockmarked. He covered this by war-painting his pockmarks in spots of white bottom-clay, so there was a snow storm raging over his face.

Taylor remembered the last time he'd seen this man, back on the agency, a few days before Loco's outbreak. Kesus always seemed to be smiling and laughing. He was gamble crazy, like a lot of Apaches, and had bet Taylor a good blanket on the outcome of a game of *wap* – where you had to throw a stick through a willow hoop being rolled along the ground. Taylor couldn't remember who'd won the game. Now Kesus lay with his chest shattered and a line of blood leaking from each side of his mouth. His lips moved slowly; Taylor leaned closer to hear.

Garth said, 'Just put a bullet for him, for Christ's sake!'

Kesus found new strength. His voice, which had been weak, now lifted so all could hear. He was speaking in Spanish.

Garth said, 'What's he saying? I only got a little cowpen Spanish.' Taylor noted an odd expression flicker over Garth's face. For one second fear might have shown there.

All of them seemed to be listening intently: Garth, Morrison, Taylor. Even Evans turned his head, very slowly, towards Kesus.

The Apache lifted his hand and pointed at Garth.

As he listened to Kesus's words, Taylor decided he'd made a mistake. He'd left his rifle half a dozen yards away, leaning against one of the Front Rocks. A mistake that put the taste of cold clay in his mouth and in his belly, and started fear humming through him. He glanced over at Morrison. The old man was staring at Kesus, frowning. Then he glanced at Garth. Taylor saw the rancher's pistol lay on the earth a few yards from his hand.

Taylor stood. He took two steps towards Garth and Morrison. That also took him two steps nearer his rifle...

Morrison reached for his pistol.

Garth was quicker. He kicked the gun and it skittered along the earth.

Taylor lunged for his rifle. He got halfway to it and froze, because Garth had his rifle levelled on Taylor's midriff. The merchant said, 'I wouldn't!'

Taylor held still.

Garth indicated with his rifle. 'Get back over there. Sit against that rock and put your hands on your head. And don't move.'

Taylor did as he was told. As he sat, he said, 'Thought it was kind of funny how that Apache hesitated before sticking his knife in you, Garth. But then again, he was surprised to find Black Shirt here. One of the two fellows who sells Loco guns! Black Shirt – that's *you!*'

Garth smiled with contempt. But when he looked at Morrison it was almost in sorrow. 'Pity you heard that, Eli. Damn shame you savvy Spanish – that's got you killed.'

Morrison glared. 'I'll be in good company! You got all those people in Devil's Pass slaughtered. And who knows how many others?'

Garth shrugged. 'Business is business.'

'You dirty son of a bitch!'

Morrison spat. Spittle caught the bottom of Garth's leg. Garth flinched slightly, and he scowled; then some of the old arrogance returned to his face.

Taylor said, 'Everybody knows nobody hates Apaches like Jed Garth. Pretty good cover for a gunrunner! I should have spotted it from the start. You knew what that Apache belt was – the safe passage belt – because you used one too, going about your business with Loco. Didn't you?'

Morrison looked to be in considerable pain from his wound. He swallowed a few times before he spoke. 'We might as well know all of it. I guess you killed Schim?'

Garth said, 'Schim was my partner in the gunrunning. He was the only one could witness against me. So, getting rid of him and pinning it on Taylor was killing two birds with one stone. Talking of which...'

Garth drifted over to the Front Rocks, keeping his rifle on Taylor and Morrison all the time. He took one quick glance out at the basin. 'Rescuers not in sight yet. Good.' Garth lifted his rifle, pointed it in Taylor's general direction. 'Looks like they'll find only one survivor of this attack!'

Evans said, 'You!'

Garth turned, and surprise showed in his face. Evans was lifting his pistol, aiming it at the merchant. His thumb worked at the hammer and his face twisted in hatred and pain.

But he was slow from his wound; he hadn't got the gun cocked when Garth fired. Evans's face dissolved in blood.

Taylor sprang to his feet. He charged at Garth.

Garth had got his rifle halfway towards Taylor, when the other man crashed into him. They slammed back against rocks which caught Garth behind the knees. He was driven beyond, on to the slope; Taylor spilled after him. Both of them went down in dust.

Slowly, they came to their knees.

Garth had lost his rifle; he glanced about him.

A few paces down slope was a dead Apache. Garth came to his feet and sprang down the incline towards the Indian. That puzzled Taylor for a second until he saw the lance lying by the dead man. A length of cane with a rusting bayonet for the head.

Taylor pushed himself upright. As Garth stooped and lifted the weapon, Taylor ran forward. He leapt from the slope, yelling. His plunging body struck against Garth and bowled him over. The two bodies, entangled, half-rolled, half-cartwheeled downslope. A minute of gouging and kicking in choking, blinding dust, then Taylor was kneeling up. He felt a bar across his throat – Garth was behind him, holding the Apache lance under his chin, yanking back, choking him with it!

Garth drove his knee into the middle of Taylor's back. Taylor's spine arched like a bow. He got both hands to the lance and tried to force it away from his throat. But Garth was stronger, the lance haft ground down on Taylor's windpipe. Breath came out of Taylor in a hoarse whine; lights flashed behind his eyes and he could feel his consciousness ebbing, his tongue forced out between his teeth. Over and behind his right shoulder, Garth gave a half-gasp, half-sigh of triumph. There was suddenly no air in Taylor's lungs, the sun flickered and was gone, he was in darkness. An instant of that, then light returned.

Taylor called on the last of his strength; he forced the haft of the lance away from his windpipe. He twisted and doubled forward; Garth spilled headlong over Taylor's shoulder. He rolled and lay on his back, upslope of his enemy, head pointing down.

Taylor tried to get up off his knees and failed. Rocks had battered him, thorns had ripped him with many small cuts. Dust seared his lungs. The Apache lance was before him. He got his hands to it but felt almost too weary to lift it.

Garth made it to his feet. He'd found another discarded weapon, this time a Winchester. He pulled the rifle into his shoulder and aimed at Taylor's face. Taylor stared at his own death, too tired and hurt to care.

Maybe the rifle was empty or jammed. Death didn't come, the weapon didn't fire. Garth took the barrel in both hands. He came at Taylor in slow, drunken strides, and then he yelled. He started to run the half-dozen yards between them, swinging the rifle as he plunged downslope. Taylor found just enough strength to lift the lance. He thrust upwards.

Impact jolted against his arms. But he felt no blow of the rifle butt, crashing against his skull.

Garth's yelling became a high, peculiar sigh.

Taylor saw that Garth had run on to the lance. The bayonet tip had entered at the base of the throat and emerged behind his head. He was dead, killed instantly, and still standing. He let the rifle drop. Then he toppled to his knees. But the lance wouldn't let him fall. The lance butt had grounded itself against the earth, the weapon propped him up. He leaned there, dead and upright.

Taylor stared at Garth in horror.

He got to his feet inch by inch. He made the slow climb upslope and re-entered the Compound.

Kesus was still managing short, ragged breaths, but the death was in his face. Morrison sat against a rock, groaning softly. He gazed at Taylor dazedly. Evans was dead.

Taylor found one of the Front Rocks to lean on. He gazed out at the basin. He heard hoofs and then a dozen horsemen issued from the east canyon and came towards him. Haze played games with them but after a little while Taylor made out Major Cameron.

Taylor looked again at the bodies strewn around the Compound. He glanced at the bodies on the slope below, the grim figure of Garth kneeling where death had taken him. Waiting buzzards circled overhead.

Well, Taylor thought bitterly, at least they hadn't gone hungry in the last few weeks. It had been a trail of death he'd followed, all the way from the Rio Grande. But a canyon wren was singing from its perch somewhere on the brilliantly coloured cliffs, reminding him that life carried on even amidst such slaughter. And there was plenty in life he still wanted to experience, from the harsh beauty of this landscape, to the music a bird made because it felt good in the morning, to the promise Taylor thought he saw in a woman's green eyes. •

The publishers hope that this book has given you enjoyable reading. Large Print Books are especially designed to be as easy to see and hold as possible. If you wish a complete list of our books please ask at your local library or write directly to:

Dales Large Print Books
Magna House, Long Preston,
Skipton, North Yorkshire.
BD23 4ND

This Large Print Book, for people
who cannot read normal print,
is published under the auspices of

THE ULVERSCROFT FOUNDATION